LAST WAVE

Paul Hayden

POCKET BOOKS

New York   London   Toronto   Sydney   Singapore

An *Original* Publication of MTV Books / Pocket Books

POCKET BOOKS, a division of Simon & Schuster, Inc.
1230 Avenue of the Americas, New York, NY 10020

Originally published in Australia in 2001 by Pan Macmillan Australia Pty Limited

ISBN: 0-7434-6472-9

First MTV Books/Pocket Books trade paperback printing May 2003

10 9 8 7 6 5 4 3 2 1

Art Direction: Deklah Polansky and Thomas Berger
Design and Illustration: Thomas Berger

Printed in the U.S.A.

For information regarding special discounts for bulk purchases,
please contact Simon & Schuster Special Sales at 1-800-456-6798 or
business@simonandschuster.com

This book is for my old man
who brought me here
and never knew what a wave could be
and now he's gone.
But told me
before he went
water will find its own level.

CHAPTER ONE

HE HOLDS MY FOOT IN HIS HAND AS HE'S TALKING to me.

"The bone is fusing itself."

"What do you mean?"

"Just what I said. The cartilage has deteriorated and because of that the bones start to rub together—and as they rub they cause a sort of sediment that actually builds up and stiffens the joint."

"*Christ . . .*" I sort of gasp quietly, and sink down a little further in the chair.

"It's a type of arthritis."

"No one's explained that properly up to now."

"Well, that's what's happening."

Right then, I'm suffering the most awful mixture of emotions. This doc is so great. He's the first one I've found that's just so calmly and clearly nailed it down for me. That's just sat there and told me what the hell's going on without all the other crap and stuffing about. And because of that I'm sort of half out of my mind with relief. I feel a little hope, a little certainty, at last. But on the other hand, now I'm really cracking up. 'Cause now I've got it square in my face how totally fucked my feet are. And I don't really think I've got a clue how to deal with it. I feel this rising fear. I don't know what they're going to be able to do. Or where that's going to leave me. And I'm only seventeen, and that's really hurting me.

I'd really done the rounds up till this guy, I think I'd seen about half-a-dozen bloody specialists. And I'd met some of the all-time champion wankers—one of them wanted to permanently fuse the bones in my feet so they wouldn't bend ever again and give me a set of walking sticks; another wanted me to get around in funny little leather boots with rockers on the bottom for the rest of my life. They'd scared the absolute shit out of me. I was cracking up. I was starting to lose hope. And then I find this guy—he's at Royal North Shore. And it's different from the very start.

I haven't been in his room for more than thirty seconds and he's got my shoes and socks off and he's grabbed a foot and he's checking it out. And it goes on like that for the rest of the consult—one foot or the other in his hands, and him working it over and pushing and prodding and really giving it the once over, while I just rave. I get going and I give him the whole tale of woe from start to finish. And he doesn't miss a beat. He just keeps on, and shoots me a question now and then—whenever he gets a gap in my noise—like, "This hurt here? How long's it felt like that there?" And when I answer, he's actually got this look on his face like it means something to him.

So I'm stoked. He's the first doc that's come at it in that way. The first one that hasn't sat behind the big mahogany desk and given me the carrot-up-his-arse routine for the first twenty minutes. The guy's an absolute legend. And I swear; there's like this lightness that begins to grow in me as it all goes along; there's this relief that builds in me as I check him out. I start to feel a little okay for the first time in quite a while. I feel like I've found someone who understands where the pain is, and what the pain is, and what can be done about it.

And the other thing that's going on, is a really weird thing. It's just this thing with someone working on your feet like that. I swear, it's totally freaky. It's the strangest feeling. It's too intimate. It's like you feel like you're sitting there in the *buff* or something—that's how it feels. It feels *too close* to you. It's this thing, as they press into the softness of your arch, as their hand works around your foot. You feel like they're getting at you where the skin is too thin. And even though you're sitting there yacking your head off—you can't ignore it, the way it feels, the way it touches a nerve. Yeah, I know I'm cracking up. I've already told you that. But I swear it's the weirdest sensation. I swear you never realize how personal a foot is, until someone grabs yours and starts working on it.

So it's a bit of a weird trip to the doc's all round. I'm sort of coming undone and over the moon all in one. So he does his whole bit, and eventually he's finished, then he gets up and goes over to his little sink to wash his hands. And I'm left sitting there, working my bare toes into the carpet pile, contemplating what a brilliant doc he is. And I'm starting to buzz a little, 'cause I'm getting just the faintest sense that maybe he'll be able to work something out here. And he comes back, drying off his hands on a paper towel, and says, "It's your arches— they're too high." Then he lobs the paper towel into the bin.

"Yeah?" I pull my foot up and take a look at it.

"Puts a mechanical stress on the front of the foot. Bit unusual in someone your age—but it can happen."

I check my foot out, I can't see it. Looks like an ordinary arch to me. I can't believe it—fuckin' seventeen and my feet are packing up. You wouldn't fuckin' credit it.

He sits back down again, in the chair opposite me, and tells me some more about it, and then starts telling me about the op he proposes.

It's really hard to explain to you the pure relief I feel then. The bastard actually has an idea about what can be done. I feel I could almost cry out loud. I could yelp with joy. I feel like I've reached the end of some kind of road at last—and I've been on my knees in the gravel all the way.

"You can't leave it the way it is," he tells me, "or the process will just continue and it'll get worse. But it's all right, what we do now is just cut the point of friction out of the joint—and it fills up in time—and you can walk fine."

"Honestly?" I say.

"Yes, honestly," he replies, with a little smile. I think he thinks I'm a bit of a nutter.

And I swear, I want to cry out. I want to leap up and hug the bastard. It's his calm way when he tells me stuff, his sureness—what's wrong, what he can do—that's what really flips me. It's like he really knows, it's like I can really believe him. It's because he's the first bastard that hasn't made me feel like I'm going to be lumping around in leather calipers for the rest of my life. I'm so stoked. I'm so rapt, honestly.

But still, I can't do it. I just can't.

I'm so stoked and relieved and thrilled—but I can't open my mouth and ask the question. It's like I'm afraid I've used up all the grace reserved for me for one day. Afraid I've got no right to any more. And I can't push it that little bit further and ask the question I really want to. The question that's there filling up every space in my head: "Will I still be able to surf?"

It's just too much. I don't do it. I wander out of there like I've just been hauled off the rocks at Anga at twelve foot after the hammering of a lifetime. And all I've got a right to, is to be glad to be in one piece. The board's smashed to bits, but I'm okay. And that's all I've got a right to. And I'm too high and grateful to ask for something more. I'm too afraid of the answer.

* * *

I head down the pub that night. Friday, Saturday—always big nights down the Steyne. Doesn't matter what else is on, you'll always find someone down there. Things always start there, no matter what else is happening for the rest of the night. Didn't even matter a few weeks back when half of us had the HSC on (the other half hadn't made it that far)—there was still always a pretty good turnout. I roll up, and pretty much the whole crew's there, sitting out in the beer garden at a couple of tables pulled together like usual. I wander over.

"Owl, what's happening mate?" The usual rave on arrival.

"Where'd you piss off to this arvo?" someone asks.

"Had to go see the doc."

"Still can't shake that dose, hey mate—told you to stay clear of those feral Queensie bitches. You'll catch yourself a fatal strain, mate."

"Or end up lookin' like Croc."

"Whichever's worse."

"Go the dose, Owl."

Hoots and snorts from around the table. More resident comedians than you can poke a stick at. Croc couldn't give a stuff. Croc'd root a dead wombat by the side of the road if he had the chance.

"Yeah, right." I grin and bear it, and get a seat and bury my nose in my schooey.

Croc's to my left, he gives me an elbow nudge. He's a big ugly bastard with a head like a potato and arms like a steve-dore. He likes to blue on the footy field, and ride big waves on the big green pin-tail gun his brother-in-law brought back from Oahu for him. I've never seen Croc back off from a swell. When the rest of us are hanging on the beach going, "Yeah, well, it's a bit big, ain't it?" and "It's a bit fucking ugly," Croc's halfway down the sand with his big green gun under his arm. He doesn't fuck around. Some guy he doesn't know drops in on him, he doesn't bother with the mouth, he just paddles straight over and punches him in the head.

"Big night tomorrow, hey Owl," he says to me, "ain't gunna miss it are ya? Haven't got something fucking terminal have ya?"

"No way, I'll be there. It's going to rip."

"The Owl's takin' the Hayls mate," Lew says, "didn't you know? He's made it sweet—he's goin' all the way, mate."

"*The Hayls?* Hayley Churchill?" Dills picks it up. "The Owl's taking the Drewester's little sister to Stink's eighteenth—no shit! How the fuck'd you swing that Owl, you sly bastard? How'd you get past her olds?"

It's like this silence suddenly falls around the table. There might be about ten guys there, the usual crowd, the hard core of the crew from down the beach, and they all go quiet. It's like, this is sort of the scoop, this is the dirt, and they're riveted. And I don't know what to say.

"Fuck, I don't know," I mumble, "it just sort of happened."

"Come on, mate, stop being so sly," Lew says. "How'd you get that hot bit of gash off the leash? Her old man's a fuckin' Nazi, he never stops heavyin'. Sees you in the street and he comes over and starts baggin' ya about your hair or the fuckin' hole in your boardies—fuckin' dickwit—thinks he's still in the army or something. Hey Stink, remember that time we're down at Manly, bastard comes out of Coles and runs into us, we go 'Hi, Mr. Churchill,' all polite and shit like that, and he just starts right in, 'What's the matter with you kids? Why don't you get your damn hair cut? How can your parents let you run around looking like that?' Rah, rah, rah, you should have heard the bastard. Tell you what, Drewe's one lucky bastard having had to grow up with that. Wonder the bastard ever made it down the beach."

"He's big time in the Manly clubbies," Poon says. "That's why he's cool with the surf—wanted Drewe to be an ace iron man."

"Bummer, hey. Wonder if he knows he rips shit."

"He sort of does," I say. "He's always been cool about Drewe and the surf. He just could never make out why anyone wouldn't want to row a surfboat."

"Fuckin what!" General howls and hoots from around the table.

"So whad'ya do, Owl, you snake—you give the old lady a box of choccies or what?"

"You'd need to do more than that—you'd need to give the old man a fuckin' lobotomy, I reckon," Lew says.

More approving hoots and cacks around the table at that one, but then it goes quiet again and it's all eyes back on me. They go silent again, waiting.

"So what's the buzz, Owl? How'd ya do it?"

"Come on, Owl—you sly dog, spill it."

"I don't know, I guess it's just kinda 'cause they know me or whatever, and that made it cool or something like that. I don't know."

Howls of disapproval and disbelief.

"Christ, I don't know," I protest. "Hayley did all the pleading and fancy footwork with them."

More howls and hoots, and I'm shat on.

I duck for cover. I head for the bar, for another beer.

Next morning, five o'clock, I'm up for the early—like always. The booze from the night before doesn't faze me. I've been chasing the early for so long now, it's like clockwork—summer, winter, whenever—every Saturday, every Sunday, for the last six years of high school at least. We drank till closing at the Steyne, then I got a ride back up the hill with Stink and Dills. We stopped in and had a bag of fries at Maccas at Fairlight with the rest of the midnight ravers—then I bailed, and weaved and wobbled my way back up my street and crashed in the front door. Lately, I like the piss a little more than I probably should. I like the dampening effect it has on the soreness in my feet. It gets in between the ache and softens it.

I leave my place in the dark, to be down the surf at sunrise. Drewe and I have worked it for years now that we try to get down there just as the lamp lights kick off along the beach. We've been meeting up for the early for so long now it's just mad. But it's just what we do. It's what we love.

To be out there, when the sun first comes, when the light's low and silvery and magic; to be drifting and moving amongst it when the swell's sweeping in and the sun's seeping thick over the blue edge of the ocean, is to be in nirvana. It makes your heart sing. To be streaming across a wall and see the light of sunrise through its glassy thickness, to push through a wave and feel its wet crashing brightness enclose you, it makes you delirious; it makes you high. It's the maddest, wildest, sweetest thing I've ever found. You end up drugged with it. You can't live without it. To take off on a six-foot set at North Steyne in the first flowing light of sunrise in spring, and drop down into a surging barreling line, with water spinning like crystal around you, and the air soft and sweet like a kiss against your skin, and the tide most of the way out so it's bowling so hard and clean over the bank you're only just making it all the way, only just hanging in there by an edge and charging so fast and nearly out of control all down the line with the lip crashing into your head—that's the thing, that I can't begin to say what it does to you, how it works you over. That's the thing that leaves you high and buzzing for the rest of the day, that rides and shoots in your blood and never fades till you finally flake that night.

I walk down the hill from my place in the early cool of the spring morning. I'm checking out the breeze, trying to feel it, thinking about the tide, trying to get a squiz at the Bower and the swell on the horizon as usual as I go. It's about 5:30 and the light's just starting to come, but it seems a little dull—there must be a little high cloud I think. On the steep bit of the hill by the Ra-Ra park I get a funny feeling, and I look around and there's a cop car there, creeping silently in the curbside, just behind me—only its parkers on—taking a look at me. I've only got my towel over my shoulder, my board and wettie are down in the garage at North Steyne where we all keep our gear. I don't give them another glance, I just keep cruising. After a little bit they slide on by me and dive away down the hill—the cop on the passenger side making a big show of taking a last good look at me as they go. I don't know what they're on about. Must figure I'm knocking in car windows or something with the towel, the wackers. But I'm not really bothered. I just keep walking and I'm looking straight out ahead, and there's an instant I suddenly realize I'm looking at the Bower and it looks like it's catching a little swell. And I forget about the cops 'cause I'm sussing the swell out and trying to figure out where it's coming from and if it's any good.

As I'm walking I'm thinking it'll be cool to see Drewe. I haven't seen him for a few days now. He didn't front last night at the pub. He didn't show at a party we kinda crashed the night before. He's on with this absolute glam babe at the moment. She's got to be the biggest put-on I've ever met in my life—all she ever does is rave about the old lady's Saab and where she's going skiing in Europe, and she dresses like a friggin' disco queen. I couldn't really give a stuff, that's all Drewe's lookout, but she's dragging him around to all the glam night spots, so lately he's not hanging out with the crew as much as usual. But he still shows for the early most of the time. So I'm thinking, it'll be cool to have a bit of a rave with him. Tell him what's been happening, and how I'm going to have the op. He's pretty much the only one I can communciate to about all this shit with my feet. I can't talk to my olds. Well, not my old lady anyway. I mumble sideways to her about it and she always gets so cut up. She reckon's surfing's the cause of it all, and that's it. She never lets up. Logically, I don't see how she could see it that way—or every fuckin' kid that ever rode a board would have this. But emotionally, she's jammed on it. Her only answer is ever: "Stop surfing, Matt. Stay off the board. That'll fix it." But that won't fix it. It'll just make it worse.

I get to the beach. The sun's just rising—a misshapen molten globe—trailing a thick tail out of the blue sea as it draws itself over the horizon. No sign of Drewe yet. There's one guy out in the water already—down at Mid Steyne, some mad bastard that just can't get enough of it. I sit on our bench, the bench the crew hang out on, and watch the break, and think about stuff, and hang on for Drewe. I've got a feeling he'll show this morning. And it feels all right to just sit there, and try and chill out for a bit. I tell you, this is it, I'm so wound up. This is the big day—tonight's the night. I'm taking Hayls to a party. And not just any party—Stink's party, his big eighteenth at the Queensie boat shed. What a blast. You know that feeling of anticipation you get where you've tee'd it all up and it's all so sweet you're only just barely hanging onto yourself—well, it's like that. It doesn't come any sweeter than this. This is it. To be taking Hayley Churchill anywhere is like a dream come true. To be taking the babe out on the first real night her olds will let her out to a party like this, is like going direct to heaven. To be thinking, I'm going to be picking her up and driving her and we're going to be together at Stink's huge session that everyone on the beach has been talking about for months, just about blows my mind so far away I don't know if I'll ever get it back. I'm so stoked. I'm going to go out in the surf and rotate.

Hayley's fifteen. I'll bullshit all my mates down the pub—but I won't bullshit you. I did squat. Hayley set it all up. Month ago, I'm down at their place, Drewe's and Hayls', one Sunday arvo after the surf, hangin' out like we always do. Drewe and I are out the back working on that old balsa gun we've been reshaping for like years now, and Drewe's old lady hangs out the back door and says there's a young lady on the phone for him. So Drewe goes off to talk to Shazza or Mazza or whatever the hell babe from amongst the half-a-dozen sorts that are perpetually chasing him, and then Hayley comes wandering out the back. Cruises out all cool and coy and divine in a funny little tube top and funny little shorts, in that way that she has—that makes it that all you can seem to do is stare at her legs, and just gawk at her in general like some kind of stunned mullet 'cause she's such an absolute bloody knockout. And she's drinking pink lemonade or something or other through a purple straw from one of those big silly plastic glasses that's nearly as big as a bucket. And all she says is, "Hey, Matt."

And I say, "Hey, Hayls."

Then, no shit, no other jazzing around, she just gets right into it, "Hey Matt, you want to take me to Pete Ryan's eighteenth?"

And you got to hand it to the babe. She doesn't hang back, she just lets you have it.

And I'm Mister Genius. I think real fast. What does this mean—the babe I've been mad stone blind infatuated with for about the last two years has seen the light and is suddenly infatuated with me? Or, Hayley wants to go to Pete's party? Hayley's fifteen and she's sick of being tied down at home by her old man who's an industrial-strength fascist, and she's such a clever bitch she's probably worked out the only bastard in the entire Manly-Warringah Shire she has half a hope in hell of getting out the front door with, is me, 'cause her olds have seen me come and go around here since I was three-quarters high to a coolite, and I'm as good as halfway to being one of the family? Yeah, I conclude, Hayley's stuck on me. The babe's finally realized what an awesome spunk I am and she can't let me go. My star-struck infatuation is being reciprocated. She doesn't really care if we go to Stink's big stir that night, that's not what it's about at all—we could go and sit in the car park at Kentucky Fried at Manly Vale and talk about the tide all night and she'd be just as blissful 'cause she's with me. Just so long as she's with me. Yup, they don't call me the Owl for nothing.

I look at her. I don't know that I can explain to you what

happens, what it is I feel, when I look at this babe. It's just a total, gob-smacked near-divinity encounter. Hayley Churchill could fart and I'd think it was perfect pitch and divine. She's got these dark eyes that are so wicked and perfect. They're the most beautiful, impish, take the absolute piss out of anything or anyone any time she pleases, divine eyes. She's got perfect skinny brown limbs, and she's just divine angles all over—her shoulders, her hips, the raise of her arse—the way she glides and bends to stretch when we're down at Fairlight Pool in the summer, before she slides into the water. She's just a fucking goddess.

"So, what do you think about Pete's?" she says. "You want a drink of lemonade?" she asks, as an afterthought.

I kind of hang there checking her out. I'm kind of in shock. I kind of wish Drewe would come back out and sort his sister out 'cause she's reducing me to rubble. I've got to tell you the truth. I'm a total dag with the babes, I'm clueless. I don't know what it is, but it's like I lack some critical skill—I just can't seem to get over this effect they have on me. They flip me out. They make me want to run for my life. I just haven't got a handle on it yet. And in my crew, hitting the end of Year Twelve, even I've got to admit that's starting to look a little poor form. Guys like Lew and Stink in the crew, they're absolute legends with the babes, they've been screwing sorts since Year Eight or Nine. But me, I'm a total fucking loss. Some sexy sort starts batting her eyes at me and I lose the plot totally. I can surf the arse out of an eight-foot Bower set—and that's probably the only thing that's saving my cred—'cause some sort starts giving me the chat and I turn into a dag.

And Hayley, well Hayley's a whole different story again. Up till Hayley I could fob it all off. I could still say to myself it just hadn't *happened* yet, so it was no sweat. I'd look at some babe and think, yeah, she's pretty cute, yeah or whatever. But no one had really knocked me off my perch yet, there was no real true ka-pow yet. So I could just keep kidding myself along, keep sort of bumbling along getting blind and falling over at parties on Saturday nights to kind of bail out of it, instead of fronting up to the sorts that were giving me the come-on. Keep telling myself because I wasn't really that hot on any of them, it didn't really matter—I wasn't really that big a lost cause. But then Hayley knocked me flat, and she really knocked me flat. I was gone. I was nailed by the goddess. So when Hayley says, "Take me to Pete's party," I'm as good as stuffed.

"So what do you say, Matt? You interested?"

"Yeah, cool. But what about your olds?" It's pathetic, but I'm trying to be as cool as I can. I'm actually trying to act like I don't know that it's that hot an idea, or whether I'm that keen on it. Where do I get this kind of talent? Some babe that I'm absolutely blind about's standing there asking me to take her to a party, and I'm standing there doing my Joe Cool routine? No fucking idea, but it's obviously a major talent, it's a bloody brain wave.

"It's all right. I've talked to them—well, I've talked to Mum—she says it's cool. I've just got to get around Dad. But he'll be cool . . . I can look after him."

I'm so dumb. I'm just hanging there. Gazing at her. Honestly, Hayley is the most beautiful creature I've ever seen in my life. And I'm so dumb, I'm honestly thinking, What does this mean? What should I say now? Does this mean she may actually like me a little? I'm just in a stupor. I haven't got a clue. I want to say, "Hayley, why me? Why ask me to take you on your big debut? Why not some other guy?" But I don't, because I'm too dumb and gutless and that's the game isn't it? She sort of acts like she kind of maybe may like me. And I sort of act like that could actually remotely, incredibly be. But no one asks, so no one gets hammered. I wimp out and play along, and she plays the bitch and plays me along for what she wants for all it's worth. And the real truth of course is, I can't tell. We can't help it, can we? People, we tell ourselves all sorts of crap. We believe what we want to believe. We're capable of believing just about anything in the wrong place at the wrong time. And at that moment, on that afternoon, I honestly didn't know. There was a part of me that genuinely believed Hayley Churchill actually wanted me—me, Matt Owen—to take her to that party. That she actually liked me, that she actually wanted something to do with me, actually me. And it wasn't just some means to an end. Some way to get what you want and from here to there. Well, like I said, they don't call me the Owl for nothing.

I'm standing there. Looking at the old balsa gun up on the shaping stand. Looking at Hayls. She's so gorgeous you want to believe anything you possibly can. She smiles so sweetly at me and turns and walks back up the path and up the steps and in the back door waving her empty lemonade bucket and saying, "See ya later, Matt." Not walks, sort of glides, or floats, or whatever it is goddesses are able to do. And I hang there by the old blank, hit by a truck. When Drewe comes back out, I'm still hanging there, not working on the board, not doing much of anything. I think I'm studying a knot in the wood, trying to remember what fucking planet I'm on.

"What's up, mate?"

"This thing's a fuckin' waste of time."

"We know that—what's your fuckin' problem?" He laughs. "We'll tart it up and sell it to some Parra—tell him it's a Duke Kahanamoku original—we'll get a fortune."

"Bullshit . . ."

"Mate, you're a glassing *ledge*—stop sweating, it's just for hoot."

"Who was that?"

"Kelly Crater—wants to know if I love her. And if I do love her, why haven't I been around to shake her peaches lately?"

"May have to tell her you've moved on, mate."

"May have . . ."

I look up at him. "Your sister's asked me to take her to Stink's eighteenth."

He smiles. "No shit . . . So she got it past the old man."

"Reckons she will."

He thinks. "She's a sly bitch. So what did you say?"

"Said I'd think about it."

He checks me out. "Bullshit."

I wander away from his scrutiny, go over and sit on the back step.

He leans on the blank and watches me.

"Mate, I don't care if you're star-struck on my sister—it's your lookout, not mine. Your judgment's fucked—but I won't hold it against you." He laughs. "I figured it was bound to happen with one of my mates sooner or later."

"Yeah?"

"Yeah. So where's it at?"

"I don't know where it's at. I'm wondering if I'm just having myself on."

"I'd say there's a reasonable risk of that, mate. I'm not going to get stuck into my sister, mate. But you know the score. Little Hayls is in it for little Hayls and no one else."

"I'm screwed. My head's rotating."

"What's the prob, bro? Stop sweating. Just ride—see where it goes. Or fuckin' give it the flick now—'cause you know Hayley, and you know the only thing you're going to get is heartache."

"Fuck, you're a hard bastard."

"Bull I am—I'm her brother. And I've seen a few, and believe me, my sister leaves them all for dead—she's the queen of vixen. She's the all-time champ."

"Well, that's it isn't it? It's different for you—you're her brother. I've got a sister and I wouldn't exactly recommend her to anyone either, but my old man's still fighting the would-bes back from the door with a stick."

"That's bullshit, mate, and you know it. Your sister's heaps older than you and it's never been the same—you've never even been that close. Hayley's always been around and we've always been like *that*. And you know what I'm on about. Hayley gets what Hayley wants."

"Okay. I still reckon it's different. I still reckon it can never be the same with a brother. You always know each other in a different way."

He looks at me. "Yeah, well, that's cool, mate, but you know the real problem—you're halfway to being her brother too. You've been to too many Sunday lunches, mate."

He shut me up with that one. He left me thinking. But it didn't change anything—Hayley got it around the old man and I was taking her to Stink's eighteenth.

CHAPTER TWO

I HEAR A CAR PULL UP. I TURN AND LOOK, AND IT'S Drewe in his old lady's old Mazda. He hasn't got his board on top, which I think is a little strange, 'cause lately he hasn't been leaving his board in the garage, and last surf we had I thought he took it home. I gaze back out at the surf and wait, then look back over my shoulder at the car, and Drewe's out and strolling across the grass.

"Hey, mate," he says.

"Hey, Drewe."

He sits up on the back of the bench alongside me. He looks pretty ratshit. He looks like he's been up all night.

"You look like shit."

"Thanks, bro."

"You on for a wave?"

He smiles wryly, watching the surf, flicking his keys over one finger in his hand. "Cop this," he pauses, "Layla reckons she's pregnant."

There's just this huge pause. This silence.

He gives a faint shake of his head and a sigh, and lifts his gaze to look out at the surf for an instant longer, then he looks at me. "How's that for an early morning ball breaker?"

"Shiiiit . . ."

"Shit indeed, mate. Last night, I go around to her place to pick her up, usual jive—out for a few drinks, maybe a bit of cha-cha, and we're driving down to the pub and she drops the bomb. I nearly ran off the road and into the fuckin' Manly aquarium. We went around to Maisy's after that and ate lentil burgers and drank rasta tea and talked it through all night. Then we went home to her place and fucked our brains out—but I tell you what, mate—it just didn't feel right." He pauses. And gives me that faint smile again. "So what the fuck do you think of that, mate? Is that a tale for six in the morning or what?"

"Faaark . . . What are you going—"

He cuts across me. "—Don't say it, mate. Don't say it, 'What are you going to do?' I've been up all night with *'What are you going to do?'* And I'm no closer to any answer. I don't have a fucking clue what I'm going to do. Not one iota. This just wasn't what I had in mind. The big plan was to surf and screw my brains out all summer and then go to art college next year. And now some babe's told me she's up the duff with mine.

Honestly—I've never been so blown away in all my life." He looks ruefully out at the surf. "Looks all right, hey. The left's working. I'll tell you what I'm not going to do, mate—I'm not going for a surf. I don't even feel like a surf—how's that for fucking tragic—and it looks pretty sweet out there. And the other thing I'm not going to do is go around sticking my dick in women quite as casually as I used to. Give you a tip, mate— think about what you're doing, before you do it—or some shit like that. 'Cause things can happen so fast you wouldn't believe it—they can leave you blinded."

He looks back out at the surf.

"You told your olds?"

"Fuck no. I haven't told anyone. I've only told you. Layla's asked me not to tell anyone—for whatever that's worth—she's not totally a hundred percent." He pauses. "We don't know what we're going to do, mate—but I'll tell you, there's not as much consolation in that as you might think."

Drewe gets up and walks over to the wall and looks down at the sand. He talks as he gazes down there. "My old man warned me, you know, mate. He kept warning me. You know the way the bastard talks—it's all building-site wisdom—*Keep your nose clean, matey. Remember, you plant, it's yours.* Well, the bastard was trying to tell me something." He sits down on the wall and looks back at me. "Layla Honso, you credit that— hot sort—easy on the eye and all that—but not the babe I was planning on having kids with or building my pole house up the coast with. Fuck mate, I don't even know how to spell 'kids.' I don't even know how to spell 'with'—it wasn't in my vocabulary. 'Well, it's in your vocabulary now, son'—as my old man would say."

He gazes back at me. He has this look on his face like it's all been expended. Like there is nothing more to say, nothing more to explain. He looks wasted. I feel the same. I have this feeling there is nothing meaningful I can ask. Drewe and I go all the way back. Back to primary school. Back to coolite kids in the South Steyne shorey. We've had so many sunrise surfs. He's simply like my brother. I have no feeling just now to run through the dumb lines. "Does she want to keep it? How do you know for sure?" I have this sense that somehow they're just not going to mean anything right now.

Drewe gazes back across the grass to the car. "Sorry mate," he says, "how ya been?"

"Not bad."

"See that new doc?"

"Yeah. He's good. I'm going to have an op."

"Yeah? Got it sorted, hey? Good stuff—you know when?"

"Pretty much soon as he can get me in."

"Things lookin' up, hey?"

"Yeah, a bit."

"I'm stoked for you, mate. It's been a bad cop." He pauses. "Still taking my sister to Stink's tonight?"

"Yeah."

"Keep an eye on her, hey? She's one of the wild things." Then he looks down at the ground, and shakes his head faintly again. "I got to go, mate. I got to get some sleep—my fuckin' head hurts." He turns and looks out at the surf. "Have a good wave, hey, bro. Looks all right—ain't this livin' in paradise fuckin' somethin'—and 'keep your nose clean.' " He smiles to himself, but he can't raise a laugh. "Fuckin' believe it?" He gets up.

"See ya," I say. "You going to show tonight?"

"Yeah, think so. See ya then, hey." He starts off, then turns again. "Hey mate—keep mum, hey. I know I don't have to tell you, but I'm tired and paranoid and I don't know what the fuck's going to happen—not a soul, hey?"

"Yeah, cool. Take it easy."

I watch Drewe back out from the beach, then listen to the familiar muffler rattle of the old Mazda as he drives away down toward Mid Steyne, the sound melting into the sound of the surf and the rising hum of the morning, until it's indistinguishable. The sun keeps coming, like it does, with that sweet radiance, that joy that it brings in the morning. In the morning it's soft and it's warm and you can almost look into its beauty. Left sitting there on the bench, alone again, I turn my face up to it and feel its first faint warmth on my skin. I go get my board and go for a surf.

I'm standing on the shore. Checking out the surf for a last time before I go in. I'm not really checking out the surf at all—I'm thinking about Hayls, and the op, and I'm thinking about Drewe. It's hard to imagine what you could do worse to rip the arse out of the way we've been feeling, the high we've been on. The HSC just finished a couple of weeks back. It's the spring. The water's warm, the air's sweet. The babes are beautiful. And we had the whole summer ahead of us to surf and party. Do a few trips up the coast—Crescent, Anga—we had it all planned. We sat down at the pub a week ago and mapped it out. Dills, Mo, Drewe and me—we were all mad keen. I didn't give a fuck about what was happening with my feet—I'd decided I was going either way. In the back of my mind I knew it was probably going to be a bit of a last hurrah, and I wasn't going to miss that. We were so set we'd as good as set the date. Drewe's old lady had given the nod on the car, we had the dough—a week riding Angourie, maybe lob up to Lennox for a day or two and sleep on the beach at Byron—we were gone. It didn't come any sweeter. And now this. I stand on the beach and I can feel some quality of expectation being sucked out of me. I stand sinking in the sand as the shorey sucks around me. It's all sort of unbelievable.

I get out amongst the waves. And it's not bad. The tide's mid low and still going out, making it a bit barrelly, it's got a bit of an edge. The surf always fixes something. You get out there and you get wet, water breaks, you push into it, you stream over it, you forget every other thing. When this shit first started with my feet I remember I used to say to myself, I don't care if they saw my damn feet off—I'll get a bloody *lid* or a bloody kneeboard or whatever, just to be out there, just to be amongst it. 'Cause that's the thing really—to be amongst it—to know that bliss when you're lost amongst that mad bright rolling blissful landscape of the surf.

I paddle out and I push through a set and feel the sun burst onto my face as I come through on the other side. My eye is caught by the vivid green of the headlands going up the coast. I slide into my first take-off, and tuck and get tight in a fast little barrel, and then thump face first into the blue silver thickness of a wall as I pull out. And dwell in brief heaven.

I hang out the back. I get a few waves. I just cruise. I can't really shake it all—there's too much. I'm feeling a little jumbled. The crowd slowly starts to roll up. Hen comes out and gets into the left just out from the pipe, and it seems that he's all cranked up this morning 'cause he's chucking wild reos all over the place and doing big gougey cut-backs like he's really amped. I paddle over to surf with him, to get a little of the vibe. Drewe's left me a little sideswiped. "Top little wave, hey Owl," Hen calls, as I paddle over. Then he turns, and slides graceful as a bird into a little unraveling left. I warm up a little more, grab a rail and get tight on my backhand a few times.

"Hey Owl, where's the Drewester?" Hen asks as we're sitting out there between sets. "He's usually on for the early, ain't he? Musta had a big night."

"Reckon so." I leave it at that. Big night—yeah, probably—they get any bigger for the bastard he's going to have to retire.

I stay out there. Surf my blues and confusion away a little.

* * *

By eleven o'clock, the whole crew's rolled up. It's that usual sprawl on the grass between the cars and the wall—boards and wetties and babes with beautiful brown limbs in bikinis, and bods crashed out after a wave and last night. I'm sitting on the bench listening to Spears and Poon and Lew conduct some rave about something or other you do to an HSV diff to make it do something or other. I ain't a car head. As long as the wheels get me down to the beach, or up the coast, I couldn't care shit. But they are. Lew particularly. He likes it low and fast and really flash. Gets it from his old man—who's got some kind of high-class workshop that only does prestige stuff, and every now and then Lew really lays it on thick and rolls up down the beach in a 244 or an E-type or whatever, and everyone goes absolutely ga-ga—particularly the babes. They spin right off their perches—half of them take one look and they just fall down panting right there on the grass in front of where he pulls in. Me, I don't know. It's my usual different view of things. If a babe gets so stuck on stuff like that that she can't see past it, then she can have it. I don't know that I could ever be that keen on a babe like that. It's just all too much of a put-on for me.

Lew can be a bit of a wanker sometimes. While ago at some party we're all at, I'm walking by and I actually hear him say to some babe, "I like my women fast like my cars." What a spiel, what a cack. I nearly walked into a lampshade it cracked me up so bad. But that's Lew, he's just one smooth bastard. And who am I to knock? Lew bulldozes the babes over so fast it's like there's no tomorrow. Anyway, they're all having this mad rave about sticking this in, and pulling that out, and super-charging some other bit, and I'm sitting there just listening for the hell of it. Then Emy Greene walks up.

"Hi, Matt," she says, "want to come for a walk up the shop?"

"Yeah, sure."

I hop down off the bench, and we go.

Emy's a pal of Raine's. And Raine is Spearsey's babe. And Raine is one of those babes of about the age of seventeen or so on this planet that for some reason I can actually hold a coherent conversation with. That is, I seem to be able to talk to the babe without totally deconstructing.

No idea how this is. Maybe it's because she's a mate's babe, or maybe I've mistaken her for a sister or something—I honestly haven't got a clue. But it really happens, I know it goes on—Raine and me, we actually talk. There's hope for me yet.

Raine tells me stuff. I tell her stuff. I work at it when I'm with Raine. I'm practicing. I'm trying to learn how to talk to girls without falling flat on my face. And she's so beautiful. Raine is from Tahiti. When I walk with Raine, it's so corny, but it makes me feel so good, so proud. I'm walking along with this babe that's an absolute angel. And you can see everyone else checkin' her out too. And she's not even noticing, she's just having a rave with me. Raine tells me about everything—like who's on with who in the crew, or who wishes they were on with who, and who's about to give who the flick, and who's totally lucking out. She tells me about stuff like what babes really like, what babes really want—and all that other shit I just can't seem to get my head around or give a rat's about it. But I care about being with Raine.

I've got no idea why she bothers, but I swear it's like she's trying to help me out or something. Maybe the rest of the crew put her on a retainer or something: "Look, just see what you can do for the poor bastard, will ya? He needs all the help he can get—and he's makin' the rest of us look bad." No idea, but we just have a rave about anything, and each time I'm with Raine it feels like something's getting a little easier. I feel a little bit looser. I feel like maybe one day I'll cut absolutely loose and do something totally radical like actually asking some babe out—or at least walk up and talk to some babe off my own bat. Who knows, anything's possible. She reckons I'm just shy. I've told her it's worse than that. I've told her I'm a social spastic.

Well anyway, that's Raine. And Emy is one of Raine's best mates from school. There's sort of three of them that hang out—Raine, Emy, and Natalie. And Natalie's too much of a blissed-out hippy chick all the time for me, and for a few other people as well, but Emy's not, she's pretty cool. She's not around much and she's sort of a recent add-on to the crew. She got down the beach a couple of times through the year, and I'd see her around, and Raine made a point of introducing us. But now school's finished she's around all the time. She's sort of fair skinned with these green eyes that you notice and long dark hair, and she's always kind of laid back and nice. We've talked a couple of times and it's always about some book she's just read or some exhibition that's on at the Art Gallery or some foreign flick she's just been to see with her older sister. She always seems to be up to something like that. And she's kind of the sort of babe that starts having that effect on me— that I-stop-fucking-functioning effect and stand there going ga, ga, ga, like when she walks up after I've just come out of the surf and she says something really sophisticated like, "Have a good surf, Matt?"

But I'm getting there. Raine's got me in therapy. Emy says, "Want to come for a walk up the shop, Matt?" And I say, "Yeah, cool." To outward appearances you could almost mistake me for normal. So we head off. Up toward the shops just over from the North Steyne club house.

And those words, *You coming up the shops?,* they're loaded with meaning, they convey one of the core rituals down the surf. It goes like this: years back, when we were little, wave-smacked, surfed-out groms, they just signaled food. "You comin' up the shops?" just flagged the post-surf pig-out. It meant a beeline to the Manly Pie Shop or Henry's or wherever, to gorge our little surf-wasted bodies. Then, as we got a little older, the message became a little more complex, it was still food, but it could be a byword for other things as well, like "Let's go check out the babes on the beach down at South Steyne," or "Let's go have a rave with the Mozzo boys," or "Let's go hang out at Mad Jackie's and play the pinnies and see what develops." And now, it has a subtle art about it, it's all in the tone. You hear Poon ask Stink if he's coming up the shops, it means Poon's scored and he wants to know if Stink's looking for a split of the mull. You hear Lew ask Maz if she's coming for a walk up the shops, it means he wants to put the hard word on her about some babe he's got his eye on—what she thinks of him, what his chances are. On the walk up the shops now is where all the politics gets done, where all the deals get made, where all the most wicked goss gets spun. It's where you find out who's doin' who, who's pissin' who off—or you can even do something really mundane like maybe haggle to buy a board, or set up your next trip up the coast. It's all sorts of shit. But it's never just to buy a sausage roll.

So Emy and me we stroll along. The sky's wide perfect blue above. The day's flooded with sun. Emy's got a batik sarong wrapped around her waist, and it sort of hugs her shape and she's kind of knotted it at the front. And she's got one of those white Indian cotton vests that's cut up high so her belly's bare. She moves with a sort of easiness, a sort of grace, like she's done a bit of dancing or something. But the thing I really like about her is she's not a raver, she's not one of these babes that's all over you with some mad babble about absolutely zero the second you see them. She's just kind of quiet and sure of herself, like she know's what she's on about.

"Go for a surf early?" she asks.

"Yeah."

"Any good?"

"Yeah, pretty good. Water's warmed up a bit." Am I smooth or what? Am I the new master of minimalist parlance with a babe or what?

"Might go in later," she says. "Much of a rip?"

"No. Not much."

"I got caught in a rip last summer, you know—at South Curl Curl. God, it was scarey."

"Yeah? What happened?"

"The lifesavers came out and got us."

"Yeah? That'd be right."

"Me and a friend of mine from school . . . We were sunbaking down at the southern end, away from the flags—we wanted to go topless. We thought we were being so cool. Then we thought we'd go for a swim—" She sort of gives a nervous laugh with the memory of it. "It didn't look that big."

"Never does."

"Yes, well, the next thing I know I'm miles out and these absolutely huge waves started coming and I honestly really thought I was going to drown . . ."

"Yeah, Curly can get pretty wicked sometimes. It gets savage rips. So wad'ya do—the clubbies bail you out, hey?"

"Yeah. They just came out of nowhere—one minute I'm going under these waves and I'm thinking I don't know how much longer I can hang on, and the next minute there's this guy with his arm around me."

"Betya he was stoked."

She just gives me a little smile, like that wasn't really a total dag thing to say.

"Boy, they told us off. They took us back into the beach and they gave us heaps. Like 'What do you think the flags are there for *little girls*?' and stuff like that. We deserved it. It was pretty close . . ."

"Yeah. You've got to watch it. I can't count the number of times I've nearly drowned out in the surf."

"Yeah, really? But never been rescued by the lifesavers?"

"No—one time the clubbies bailed me out. I was a little grom down at South Steyne and it was too big for me and I started heading for New Zealand—the clubbies came out and hauled me in. They're all right. They just really piss us off when they take our boards."

We walk along.

"You going tonight?" she asks.

"Yeah."

"Raine told me you're taking Hayley Churchill."

"Yeah."

And there it is, splat. There's kind of a big pregnant pause. But I'm checking her out, and she doesn't look pissed, she looks something else. Then she hits me with it.

"How come?"

How come? What the fuck does she mean "How come?" 'Cause the babe's madly wrapped in me of course. What the fuck's with everyone, haven't I got any cred at all? Why's everyone acting like me taking Hayley anywhere is one big fucking fat joke? 'Cause I guess it is.

" 'Cause she asked me to," I say. And I draw a sweet moment of pleasure from that reply. It comes out of me so honestly and directly, to her, who I'm starting to realize I like an awful lot.

"Do you like her?"

Do I like her? Shit, this babe's tough. She throws another one like that I'm going to hit the deck.

"Yeah." I do it again. I just say it, true and straight and simple. I figure it must be Emy, she has some mesmerizing effect on me. She's like a truth serum.

"Does she like you?"

Aw, come on. Give me a break. What the fuck is this? Are you going to start beating me about the head next?

I don't say anything.

"It's just that you don't seem her type, you know. I was kind of surprised when Raine told me. She's a bit of a bitch. Well, she's a bit of a bitch from what I've seen of her at school anyway . . ."

"Yeah. Well. We've known each other for heaps. I've been surfing with Drewe for years. And she wanted to go to Stink's party."

And God, I don't know what I'm doing. Honestly, I don't. I feel like I'm betraying some part of me, all that madness in me that's longed after Hayley for so long. But at the same time, it feels all right. It feels like I just can't *not* do this. Like I can't let it happen in any other way, or I'd be denying some other part of me, that's *only* me.

She walks along. Quiet. Not fussed. I'm looking at her from the side. She has this pretty little nose that sort of turns up and has a couple of freckles on it. I'm thinking she probably hates those freckles. And I'm thinking I'm starting to get some kind of idea about the babes. Her hair is dark and long, and it sort of drifts at the edges as she moves. I keep watching it do that, and it has this mesmerizing effect on me. It's so beautiful. I'm kind of entranced I'm so close to it.

"I like your hair."

"Why, thanks," she says. She seems a little surprised. "But it's the wrong color, right?"

"What do you mean?" And I'm actually not playing dumb here. I'm actually really this dumb. It doesn't occur to me right off what she's on about.

"You know . . . it doesn't bleach blonde . . ."

"You want to be blonde?"

She laughs. "No. But don't you have to be a blonde . . . you know . . . to be a *surfie babe*?"

"You want to be a surfie babe?"

"Not really." She grins.

"Well, that's cool with me." And it occurs to me that doesn't mean a fuckin' thing. "I still like your hair."

"Thanks."

"You going tonight?" I ask.

"Think so. Just trying to arrange a ride. Nat might drive. I don't like bugging Raine and Sean all the time."

"Raine wouldn't mind."

"I know. But I can't ask them to take me home. They want to go off and do their own thing."

We walk. My gaze drifts up for an instant toward the sky, which seems to have faded, to a paler metal blue. And I go off the track for a bit, the wide stunning beauty of the sky draws my thoughts in a strange way. These things, in this place where we live, we soak them up. They flood into us. In this place the light is so stunning, it never stops amazing me, filling me up and overwhelming me. I look down from the sky, and my eye is caught by a patch of silver-white light dancing out on the surf like a shoal of fish.

"I'd offer to take you if I could," I blurt out. It actually comes out like that. I think it actually makes sense. I think I owe Raine about five hundred bucks in consults.

"That's sweet, Matt. Thanks."

And that's the bit that really spins me, the way she says "That's sweet." It's one of those things that you can say in ten different ways—it can be one of the most puerile and meaningless things a babe can utter to you, or it can be so true and sincere it's like an arrow into your heart. And she's done it, she's pierced the flesh.

She looks sideways at me and just gives me a little smile. I feel this throb in my crotch. I get this flash in my head. This vision. I can feel myself up against her. Feel her thighs through her thin wrap, feel her belly pressed against me, feel her arse, her chest, my hands against the shape of her back. I'm walking along with her and I start getting a hard-on. I'm spinning out totally. Thank God we make it to the shop.

"You getting a drink?" she asks.

"Ah, yeah—*no*—I don't know. I just came up to be with you. I've already been up earlier . . . doesn't matter."

"Cool," she says, like all that was perfect wisdom.

We're standing at the entrance to the shop, we've sort of stopped in the doorway, and she's standing facing me, real close to me, 'cause the doorway's sort of jammed us together a little I guess, and she's watching me. And she just pauses there. And then she rises up and leans into me, and she kisses me. And I swear the essence down through the center of me dissolves in a rush. I swear they blow the whole fireworks truck up in my head in one go. Her lips are so soft and taste like sweet tea. And then I kiss her back. Then we stop and she sort of lowers back down and we stand there in the doorway looking at each other. And she smiles.

"Again?" she says really soft to me, and I see for the first time that she has sort of honey flecks in the green of her eyes. And I lean forward and we kiss again. And I swear, I can feel the world flowing on its axis.

"*Hey! You two!* What the hell—*cut that out!*" It's mad Polish Jackie, goin' right off. "What the hell you two playin' at! Jesus H. Christ, Mr. Matt! What's the story, son! Leadin' a girl astray this time in the morning? Scarin' the payin' customers!" Jackie's really whuppin' it up. He's snappin' and thumpin' his tea towel on the glass counter as he raves; wavin' his big white arms madly about as he gives us heaps.

I just look at Emy. "You still want a drink?"

She smiles at me. "Yeah, sure. I'm not scared of him."

I follow her inside, grinning like a moron at Polish Jackie. And thinking, she's not scared of anything. And watching the contour of Emy's arse through the fine cotton of her batik wrap and thinking how good it looks. And thinking, *oh Christ . . .*

We walk back up the beach toward where the crew hang out.

"Thanks for the ice cream, hey," I say.

"Can I have a bite?" she asks.

I stop, and hold it up to her. She's so close when she bites it and she puts her hand on mine to still it, and I swear, oh God, she's just the most beautiful thing. I swear my head's spinning and my heart's surging.

"I've been thinking about you all year," she says, as she's up close. "Do you know that? Do you remember last summer, the first time I came down with Raine—it was at the end of the summer, just before we went back to school?"

"Yeah?"

"Do you really? I don't believe you. What color costume did I have?"

"Red. And the top was a bit too . . . it looked sort of . . ."

"—Big. Oh God—you noticed that! How could you say

that! Oh God, how embarrassing . . . I'm going to kill Raine—she told me it looked fine . . ."

"It did look fine. It looked great. I just noticed . . . I shouldn't have said that . . ."

We're nearly back to the crew. "I've got to split now," I say. "My old man wants me to help him move some stuff."

"Okay."

I stand there dumb. Real dumb. I don't have a fucking clue. I don't know what to say. There's this thing with Hayley. And now this with Emy. I feel like I've gone from zip to breakneck in a nanosecond. I'm cracking up.

"Emy. Look . . ."

She smiles at me. "What is it about the way you say my name . . . I like it."

"I love it—'Emy'—it's so perfect."

"Yeah? No one's ever said that."

Shit, I've lost it again. I'm stuffed. I'm going to go and live in a Tibetan monastery or something.

"Matt."

"Yeah."

"It's cool. I understand about tonight."

"Cool."

And I'm not sure I even know what's been said, what's been meant. But I can't say more. It can only be left.

"And maybe I'll see you tonight anyway, hey, if Hayley Churchill doesn't demand every instant of your time or something like that, you know . . ."

She's a wicked bitch. They're all wicked bitches—I think I'm starting to know something.

"Cool." Back to that. Minimalist communication. No risk of saying anything that might actually give something away or stuff something up or actually mean too much of anything.

We're still standing there. Looking at each other. I've finished my ice cream. She's still looking at me. Kind of with that funny, perky, you're not really sure if she's taking the piss or not smile of hers.

"Emy."

"Yeah."

"You're something, you know."

"Yeah?"

"You're so gorgeous."

"But what about my mind?"

"Your mind's gorgeous too."

"My aunt says the sexiest thing about a person is their mind."

"Yeah—she says that?"

"You want to kiss me again?"

"We'll cop heaps if we do, everyone can see us."

"Who cares?"

"Not me."

"Yes you do. I can see you do. You look like you're going to split and run any second now."

I shut her up good. I lean forward and kiss her. I even put my arms around her this time. I go the whole way. I can feel the heat of her belly, of her chest, rising up against my front. I can smell the perfume of all of her.

We stand there in the sun and kiss a little. It feels so good you don't want to stop. Some kid goes by along the path on his bike and rings his bell at us.

Boy, do we cop it from the crew. You could probably hear the hoots all the way down to South Steyne the way they start carrying on.

I duck for cover. I get my board and get out of there.

CHAPTER THREE

I'M IN THE KITCHEN, EATING A CHICKEN SANDWICH for lunch. My old lady and my sister are there. They're giving me heaps.

"He's taking a *girl*."

"A *girl!* My God! What's she look like—two heads or what?"

They've got this thing about me and girls. They reckon I don't tell them anything, they reckon I haven't got a clue. They're spot on on both counts.

The scheme of the politics in my family has always been a little skewed—like everyone else's, I guess. There's always been an odd sort of alliance between my sister and my old lady, a sort of an alliance by default—'cause they've got nowhere else to go. 'Cause the fact is, me and my old lady Delia, well in some ways, we couldn't be further apart a lot of the time—in the things we want, the way we see things. I love her heaps, like you do your old lady, but the way I see it, she can be the all-time champion put-on at times—and I just run a mile from that. For me, the only genuine common ground in our house seems to be between me and the old man. We don't say much, but I get this feeling we always seem to understand where each other's at. We just cruise.

"She's not ugly at all," my old lady says. "She's Drewe Churchill's little sister—she's a very attractive young lady." This is like a first, I nearly choke on my chicken sandwich—my old lady's saying something positive about what I'm doing.

"Drewe Churchill's little sister? Hayley? You're taking Hayley Churchill out?"

"To a party, yeah." Chicken sandwich in my mouth. Another bite. Stuff it in. Get the Christ out of here. Why the hell aren't you two old dears out buying shoes like usual, instead of in here bugging me? And stuff that up your jumpers anyway—yeah, that's right, that luscious tart Hayley Churchill. What's it fucking got to do with you anyway?

"So who's party is it?"

"Some guy's."

"Did you hear that!" Delia cuts loose.

Swear, I can whip her into a frenzy in three seconds flat.

"*Some guy's.* Where are you going? *Out.* Who was that? *Just a friend.* It's like pulling teeth."

No it ain't, it's what comes naturally. But Delia doesn't appreciate that. And big Sis only makes it worse—she's the tell-all girl. Where he works, what he earns, whether he's got a pimple on his arse, what his dad makes, what his mum does—the whole kaboodle in fine detail. No wonder I get them in a spin.

"Well, at least we know it's some guy's," big Sis says, "you know, like it might have been the Dalai Lama's or maybe Frankie Avalon's—you never know . . ."

"The Dalai Lama's having a party—I didn't know that."

"Oh, don't even try to be funny. It's less than pathetic."

"You should know—you're the social register tart."

"Don't you dare talk to your sister like that," Delia jumps in. "And we should know better than to try and get any information out of *him*—he never tells me anything. I ask him where he's going and all I get is *out*."

I laugh. I reckon that's funny. Seems funny to me.

Delia winds up. "That's not funny. Your mother has a right to know where you are. What if something happens? What if you get hurt or something? What if you drown? It's like the way you disappear down the beach at all hours of the day and we don't even know where you're going."

"Depends on the swell."

"*Depends on the swell!* Don't give me that rubbish. What is a swell? And why does it possibly depend on it?"

My old lady's not keen on the surf, never has been. Tennis is the game. From day one the surf made her real nervous. "Don't you come home if your leg gets bitten off by a shark!

Don't you come home if you drown!" Wouldn't dream of it, Delia—I'd quite happily just wash up on the shore. I'm an immense disappointment to the poor dear. She's a tennis player. She's big big time up at "the club"—pristine tennis courts, crisp little white skirts, downey little white socks with little pompoms at the back, swimming pools, eighteen holes, gin and tonics—more cravats than you can poke a stick at. I'd rather wash up on the shore with a leg missing. I'm a saltwater ratbag down to my core, and proud of it. Christ, she's even on the social committee. I can't imagine the embarrassment she's suffered. Well, no, I can—she's told me. "Does your son play, Delia?" "Well, no—" Oh the horror, oh the ignominy. "He, he . . . arrgghh . . . he surfs." I suspect she doesn't even get that last bit out. She probably tells them I'm in a wheelchair or something. It's so hard on the old lady, she wanted one of those white-socked, clean-cut, square-jawed all-Australian tennis boys for a son. We've got a couple of them at school—Croc seems to delight in thumping them now and then on a purely arbitrary basis. I think they're just so peachy and squeaky it gets up his nose. Think I kind of know how he feels.

For a while there, early on, there was a bit of a war, a bit of a campaign: "Be home at ten so you can come up to the club for some tennis lessons." It was fairly early in the bit, early high school—she hadn't given up hope yet. So I'd get up at four so I could get a couple of surfs in before I obediently dragged my arse home. I'd make it to the club, but I'd wear black socks and my shittiest old wax-head T-shirt and snarl at any little tennis dweeb that attempted to talk to me. And spend the morning watching the clubhouse flags to work out if the wind had changed and the surf had turned off-shore. Fuck I hate tennis. The old lady gave up in the end 'cause I think the embarrassment, the damage to her image, started to exceed her ambition. She gave up, but I still get the odd sly maneuver now and then. She's gotten wiser, it's a much more subtle campaign. She brings her friends' daughters home from the club now and then—and some of these daughters are real honeys. "Matt, come and meet Lisa. Lisa and her mum have just dropped in for a drink before they go home. This is Lisa, she's from the club. She plays in the A squad on Saturday mornings. They just came back from Nouméa." Hi, Lisa, you look sweet. No offense, but I'm conducting the hundred years war here with the old lady and you'd do well not to get in the middle of it, and there's no way I'm showing any interest in you or that friggin' game you play. I'll impale myself on the nose of my surfboard first. "Hi, Matt. You play tennis?" "No fuckin' way—can't stand the game—full of pratts." She'll stop bringing them home eventually.

But there's some consolation—big Sis is Delia's salvation. She's the sparkling A-grade girl. Got through to the state finals a couple of years back.

My old man comes in and rescues things. "Hey, Matt. Ready to roll?"

"Yeah. What are we doing?"

"Bunch of desks—from the office at Kirribilli—over to the office at Drummoyne."

"He's taking a *giiirl* out tonight—did you know that?" big Sis tells the old man.

"Yeah, anyone we know? Not one of those airheads from the club I hope."

I just crack up. I got to hand it to my old man. God, he's a killer. He's a cack. Every now and then he lobs one into the middle. He gives 'em heaps, and they've got to cop it sweet 'cause he's the one that coughs up on the fees. And Christ, he probably really knows how dire it is up there—'cause the old lady drags him up there and makes him play a game now and then. But not often. I think the deal actually is: I'll only pay the fees so long as you don't make me go near the place.

"As if any of them would go out with him—"

"As *if*," I chortle.

"You be quiet—he's going out with a perfectly nice young lady—Hayley Churchill."

The fact that my old lady seems to approve of Hayley only seems to forbode in my mind that the whole thing is absolutely and horribly doomed. And what about Emy. Should I tell them about Emy too?

"Wonder if he's going to comb his hair?" Sis shoots.

I finish my sandwich. "Hadn't thought of that. What do you reckon, Dad? Comb the hair or not?"

"You go out of here without combing your hair, young man, and I'll . . . I'll . . ." Delia really can't help it, she takes the line so hard sometimes you could lose an arm.

"Ah, yeah?" I stop, I'm standing at the door with my old man, we're about to go. I'm actually, genuinely kind of interested. What is it Delia will do to her lost-cause surfie son if he doesn't comb his hair? Confiscate his board like one of the bloody clubbies? I nearly cack myself thinking about it—I get this vision of me out in the surf and my old lady running up and down the beach blowing the clubbie whistle: "Right, that board rider in the blue wetsuit—come in, your board's gone for a week—you haven't combed your hair." I swear, I'm cracking up.

"—I'll phone Hayley's mother and tell her not to let her daughter out."

"Cool with me. Plenty more fish in the sea."

"*What!*" I hear them howl behind me.

And I'm gone. I bolt big time. Through the gap, and out of there.

I flee down the front path pursued by a hail of screeches from Delia and the big Sis. "Did you hear him! Did you hear what he said! He thinks all women are fish!"

"You're pushing your luck, mate," my old man says, as he gets into the rental ute beside me.

As we're riding over to the office I make the connection. It's like for the first time it occurs to me. I swear, I couldn't be much dumber. "Hayley Churchill's old lady is in the club?"

"Eileen Churchill? Think so. But I'm not really up to speed with things up there."

"Can't imagine why."

"Matt, strange as this may sound, keeping your mother happy actually has some value in this world."

I shoot him a look. "Yeah, I'll keep that in mind. How's the boat?"

"Up on slips this morning—they're working on her now—should be off by tomorrow. Looks pretty good. When are you coming for a sail?"

"When I can't surf anymore."

He draws breath and gets this sort of far-off pained look. It's a look he gets any time there's any discussion about my feet. He was a bit of a sportsman, still is. He feels it, he understands it, the way you suffer a breakdown of a part of you. How it digs into you. The way it takes away what you love.

"So how are they going?"

"Okay. Still giving me a little grief. But I'm hanging in there."

"You seem a bit happier after seeing that doctor yesterday."

"Yeah, heaps. I reckon this guy knows what he's on about."

"You still riding your board?"

"Pretty much. I'm just hanging back a little. Acting like an old fart on a mal or something."

That raises a grin from him. He's been threatening to get a mal and get out there and waste me for years now.

"So what happens after the operation?"

"He says we have to wait and see."

"That okay with you?"

"Don't think I've got much choice. But whatever this guy does—I reckon it'll be the best you can do."

He nods.

We drive for a bit. We go down over the Spit Bridge and he's checking out all the boats, and who's on the water, but he doesn't say anything. That's what I like about my old man, he does his own thing but he doesn't ram it down your throat. The more I see people, the more I appreciate that.

"It may be a bit tough," he says, "the way you're going to have to come to terms with things. It's like a footballer doing his knees and his career's over."

"Well, I'm glad I'm not first grade, or I don't think I could hack it."

"I don't know if it's the first grade bit that matters, Matt—I think it's just how much you love the thing. You love surfing like a first grader."

"Yeah."

My old man's been there. He played colts and reserves right the way up through the Manly Ra-Ra ranks. He's sailed in more than a few Sydney-to-Hobarts. He understands the mad passion for these dumb-arse things. The way they get in your head, and really do it over.

"Keep me up on things, hey, Matt. Let me know how you're going. If you start having a problem—even a little problem— let me know, hey."

"I will."

"This thing tonight, you driving?"

"Yeah."

"Take it easy, hey."

"I will. I always do."

"I know you do. And I hate to harp—but it's tough around your age, mate. I know, I've been there—everyone's blowing their brains out. Just try and play it cool."

"Yeah. I will."

"How's your mate Drewe?"

"He's fine." *Shit yeah*, he's having a baby.

We drive out to Kirribilli and load a bunch of desks into the ute, then we take them over to the office in Drummoyne. We get back about four. The wind's swung off shore—warm and dry from the nor'west, and I'm thinking about going for a late wave as I walk up the path. I tell myself that's dumb. I tell myself to save a little for Stink's party and tonight. But I'm too amped. I've got to shake it out. I'm thinking about Hayley. I'm thinking about Emy. I keep getting this picture in my head of Drewe cradling a baby in his arms. I'm starting to trip out. I get my gear and head down for a quick one. I want to burn it off.

I drive down the beach. It's getting lateish. The light's still good, but everyone's gone. Except Drewe. He's sitting on the bench we hang out on, on his own. I park the car and walk over.

"Hey, mate."

He turns. "Matt. How's it goin'?"

"Good. What's happening with you?"

"Nothing, mate. She's preggers, that's it."

"You do another test?"

"Yeah. Today. Went to the chemist with her to buy it. Then

back to her place. Tell you what mate, I've never had so much fuckin' fun." He pushes his tangled hair back behind one ear, and gazes down at nothing on the grass. "What a blast."

I just hang there and check him out for a minute. This whole thing is the biggest head spin. This is Drewe. Drewe is the guru. He's the local nass. On the beach from South Steyne to Queenscliff there's no one I reckon that rides better. And there's more than a few that reckon the same. While the rest of us sort of strive to be radical, to pull things off. Drewe's way past all that, he's all fluid and loose and soaring. He does stuff you never even thought possible. He takes a take-off so late out at the Bower at low tide over Surge you watch him and think that's not doable—you can't get the board up, you can't get it round. But he does. He kind of shows the rest of us there's another plane you can take it to that we barely even know exists. Two years ago he got a sponsorship for his boards. Last year, a sponsorship for his wetsuits. The powers that have an interest are subtly nudging him toward the Aussie Tour—no matter how much he's always been more *soul* than *comp* surfer. He's a little like the local legend—to say the babes fall at his feet and half the guys on the beach are awe-struck wouldn't be an overstatement.

"So what now?"

"She's sort of driving it, mate. We're going to wait and see. She doesn't know what she wants. I don't know what I want. I'm treading water, mate. I'm in the rip and I've busted my leggie and lost my board and I'm just hanging there—"

"—wondering if the best thing to do is get sucked out to sea?"

He laughs, "You said it, mate." Then he looks over at me again. "Mate, can you get your head around it? There could be a little kid running around next year—and it could be mine. I'm only fucking eighteen."

"Said it in one, mate."

He laughs again. "Fuck. I've got to get some waves in while I can. Let's go, hey."

"Bower might be on?"

"Yeah. Looks all right, hey, tide's right—I've been checkin' it out while I was sitting here contemplating my future—looks like the swell's hooking into it a little."

"Take your car, hey?"

"Yeah. Go get your gear. Let's go."

I go over to the garage and get my board and wettie.

The Bower's special. It has a special place in our surfing psyche. It has a thing, an aura, that's developed over the years. It's an accumulation of all those perfect twilight surfs spinning around the bright rock of the headland; all those big, big, thumping winter days when it was where you headed 'cause it was one of the few places that could hold the swell. It's all those long blue double-peaked Bower walls you've set up on and looked down the line of and just gone, Oh my God. It just keeps building in our hearts. When it's going off, I reckon it's the best wave on the Northern Beaches. And now we sort of save it. We don't go all the time. We don't bother if we think it's only half working. We wait, and we know it will come—another day, maybe in the winter, when the offshore's lashing the spray like ice across your face, and a monster Tasman swell's sweeping in from the south. And you're out in the channel, watching a thick, throwing out, absolutely monster lip thunder and spit its way around the headland, with the purpled-red rock backdrop of the cliff face behind. You know it'll happen again. And you know you'll be out there. And it all just keeps piling up, in this place where we keep it. For me and Drewe, it's some kind of nirvana.

We drive around through Manly and up the East Hill.

"You're dropped in the poo, mate," Drewe says.

"Yeah, what I do?"

"Blower started going beserk at home this arvo—all the fanny club with hot tales for Hayley about some babe they reckon you were rubbing up against down the beach this morning."

"Yeah—that right?"

"Sure is. So what's the story?"

"I don't know. I'm down the beach this morning. I go for a walk up the shop with Emy Greene, and next thing I know she sort of jumps me . . ."

"*She sort of jumps me . . .* Are you for real, mate?" Drewe's cacking himself. "Mate, you kill me . . . So what's the story—you keen on her?"

"Yeah."

"And what about Hayls?"

I think. "Shit, I don't know. I don't know what the fuck's going on. I think I've lost the plot."

"Listen, mate, it's no skin off my nose. I couldn't really give a stuff one way or another. But I'll tell you, you really stirred the possum today . . ."

"Yeah?"

"Yeah. There's hope for you yet. Just don't get anyone up the duff, hey. I highly unrecommend it."

"Where's Layla at?"

"She's freaking out. She's afraid someone's going to find out."

"Like who?"

"Like everyone. Like her olds, like her friends, like the Pope. She doesn't want anyone to know. She's spinning. She's a real paranoid babe all of a sudden."

We're following the road that snakes around above the bay, past all the big houses and out to the headland.

"She was going to do Law wasn't she?"

"She's still going to do Law—far as I can see."

"She pissed?"

"Mate, she couldn't be more pissed. She was on the fucking pill she reckons. How can you be on the pill and get up the fucking duff! And she's extra pissed at me—reckons I've got some kind of wonder dick that can shoot holes in the pill."

"She's really pissed with you?" I ask.

"Yeah. *No*. I don't fucking know. You know what fucking Layla Honso's like—she wants to rule the world. I just want to go to art college and design labels for baked bean tins. You know how fucking funny she thinks that is? She thinks every guy should be a merchant banker like Daddy."

"I always thought she was a pain in the arse."

"Now you tell me, Owl buddy."

"Ain't my beeswax. So I don't really get it? What's the problem? Haven't you really already got it worked out?"

He sighs and sort of hunches over the wheel a little. "No. We don't know what we want. She's got a moral issue. She's got a huge moral issue. And I don't know what the fuck I've got."

I feel this huge really idiotic urge to burst out laughing. I think Drewe detects it.

"Go on, mate, laugh. Must be one big cack from where you're sitting. But I'll tell you what, it's pretty fucking heavy duty from over here. Fucking Layla Honso—it was like, yeah, just for the spin, couple of months max—the babe's got a set of jugs on her that would make the editor of *Playboy* weep—and talk about a cranking in the sack, mate, there've been times I haven't been able to see straight for two days. But it was always going to have a short life—even for her. And now this."

"How the fuck can you get a babe pregnant when she's on the pill?"

"Don't you fucking start!"

We pull into the car park at the Bower. The car park faces east and sits right on the edge of the headland. It's my all-time favorite car park on the planet. Middle of winter, you swing into the Bower car park and you can see the whole lot, spreading out before you—the great vastness of the winter Pacific, it just goes and goes, spreads and swirls, for miles and miles away before you. And you get a view of the swell, of what's happening, like you get nowhere else. I could sit there for a week and not get bored.

"Let's go check it out, hey," Drewe says.

We leave the car, and walk out the path that runs though the bush to the crest of the headland where it overlooks the break.

We stand there on the edge of the big bald rocks looking down, like we've done a hundred times before. There's a couple of guys out. It's smallish but it looks worthwhile. Tide looks about right, it's sucking, but not too much. There's a nice little wall pushing through the Racecourse—but probably not enough size for Winky.

"Looks all right."

"Yeah."

"Want to take a seat for a bit?" Drewe asks.

"Yeah, sure."

We sit on the edge of one of the great sandstone rocks that crest the headland. The closer I look at Drewe I realize he's looking a bit ratshit. We sit there and are silent and just check it out for a bit—the great expanse of the bay over to Queenscliff headland, then all the beaches and headlands running north, right up to Palm Beach—running into the heat haze if you can see that far. The sun's low—over a little south of west, getting thick and yellow as it settles into the haze.

"If a babe gets the runs," Drewe says, "that's how it can happen apparently. It can stop the pill from working."

"Shit that's a new one."

"No it's not. Chemist told us. It's on all the packets."

"So is that what happened?"

"I don't know—Layla doesn't know. But it can happen. And I never thought it could—I thought the pill was one hundred percent."

I sit there, my legs pulled up, my arms around them, taking in the big sweep of water and light that falls away before me, and listening to Drewe.

"Fuck, my old man shits me. You know what one of his favorite expressions is? 'Nothing's a hundred percent.' You know the number of times I've heard that bastard say that, and I've thought, Christ, what's he crapping on about now."

Drewe laughs. A sort of tired bark. "Can't you fuckin' see me in a couple of years, mate? *'Nothing's a hundred percent junior—and don't you forget that.'* " He lets out a long, crazed sigh. "Oh God, I'm fucked. I feel like my life's turned to liquid shit overnight."

I'm searching for something to say to him. But I'm not finding it. I feel completely not up to it. I've known the guy since primary school and now he's cracking up and I really don't know what to say or do or how to help him out. I'm so far out of my depth it's tragic—I haven't even gotten laid yet, never mind have advice on hand to give when you get some babe up the duff and it's the last thing you want.

"So what happens?"

"What happens? Layla's going to do some yoga and she's going to think about it. Then we're going to talk about it some more. Those were her actual words: 'I'm going to do some yoga and think about it.' " He throws his arms out at the panorama before him and yells, "Mate, what was I doing screwing that sort. I must have been out of my mind. '*Don't let a sort's jugs get in the way of your judgment.*' That's what I'm going to tell my son. Fuck. 'Nothing's a hundred percent'—I'll let his grandpa serve him that one up."

He folds back in a little. He looks exhausted. He's looking out at the water. "You know what it is, Owl. I think I'd keep it, and she wouldn't. If it was me—I think I'd keep it. I don't think I could end any living thing. I'm just like that. I know women abort and miscarry and have dead babies and all that shit all the time—but I'd still keep it. Maybe that's why. That's what it is, mate. It's a child, and I kind of respect that. I don't care if I'm eighteen or what. I don't give a fuck if we live together or not. But I think I want to keep it. It's just sort of the way I am, it's in my nature." He's lowered his voice and it's sort of soft. He looks at me. "You know what I'm saying?"

"Yeah."

We pause.

"But it's not *you* . . ."

"No. It's Layla. And she calls it. She's carrying it." He smiles to himself. "You know, mate—I feel closer to my old man than I ever have in my life. Isn't that the fuckin' weirdest thing to say? You know how it's been—that lumpy old bastard and me have been at each other hammer and tongs since I was five—but all this shit has made me see him in a way I never dreamt was even possible."

"Why don't you talk to him?"

"I couldn't, mate. I fucking couldn't. I couldn't bear the shame. He'd take the piss out of me so hard I'd never live it down."

"You don't know."

"No. I know."

"Well, maybe this is different."

We sit and watch the water, which has grown more orange with the sky.

"It's not just her decision, mate," I say.

"I know, mate. But that's not an easy part of this."

We go get our boards and go for a late wave in the sinking metal-blue light. I feel a sort of completeness being out in the surf with Drewe. I can surf alone, I can surf with anyone else, any time. But it's been a routine with Drewe for so long that when he's not around out there I feel like there's something missing. Out in the water I've been looking around for him, checking out what he's doing for so long it's just a habit. I've learned this ease about the freakish way he can ride. It still blows you away. But you get the hang of it, you acquire a sort of nonchalance, and just hang back and enjoy it. Like the way he can come backhand off a lip—he's one of those guys that really lays it back on the bottom turn, so he slingshots up into the lip—and for an instant he's hanging there right upside down vertical, his arse literally higher than his head—then gouges the biggest fucking reo. I've seen him do it in fuckin' eight-foot fuckin' North Narra, just watched and your heart stops 'cause you're going, Aarrgghh—the boy's insane—he's going to get absolutely smashed, and then he lands, and you can never fuckin' believe it. You kind of get the hang of that sort of shit.

We paddle out from the old dock at the foot of the headland and get a few waves. It's only about two to three and pushing a little bit too much from the east, but it's good enough to be worth it. I tuck into a few of those thick blue Bower pockets and try to charge it from behind second peak a couple of times. I make one and get my arse totally kicked on a couple of others, but it's not big enough that it hurts. It's all just got that sweet feeling of release you get when the water shakes you. Everything else just gets washed away. You forget.

And between sets, I sit out there on my board, dipping my feet deep down into the translucent green, searching for the farthest, coolest parts of the aqua—to chill a little of the ache out of them.

After a few waves we're sitting out the back. The water's so clear and the air's so sweet and orange and pale, and the sky's so blue it makes you sick. I'm just hanging out there soaking it up. I think Drewe's doing the same thing. He doesn't look like he's going anywhere.

"So what's the dirt on this scuttle about you and Emy Greene, mate?"

"Scuttle, mate."

"Yeah—that's it—you're being awful foxy, mate. Jeez, my poor l'il sister's going to be heartbroken when she finds out her big date really was wandering around North Steyne this morning, sticking his tongue down the throat of any stray bit of talent that came along."

"It wasn't like that—I don't know what happened."

"We never know *what happened*, mate. And what about my poor l'il sister, hey, we all know what a sensitive little thing she is."

"Yeah right."

"If it wasn't for the fact she was such a major-league bitch, a big brother might be worried for her interests."

"Yeah right again, mate."

He drifts over a little nearer to me. "Mate, what are you doing? The girl's not your speed—she's royal pain in the arse material. All her and her little gang can talk about is Lew and Stink and Jacker Milton and suede heads like that. Why are you wasting your time?"

"I don't know. I kind of like her."

"Well, she doesn't give diddley about you, just in case you've got any doubts, mate. She's just after a ride."

"I know."

"Then why bother?"

"I don't know."

"Nothing's going to change. And what about Emy, hey? Don't blow that, hey. She's a fuckin' nice babe. You going to let little Sis screw that up for you sweet—'cause you give her the opportunity and she will."

We hang there in the water a little. The wind has faded, it is absolutely still.

"What are you doin', mate?"

"I don't fuckin' know. Don't ask me."

"Cool. I won't. I just wanted to let you know—Emy Greene's a really nice babe, and my sister's not—she's just a full-throttle powerbitch."

"Long as you're sure you've got her sussed, mate."

"I have got her sussed. I've been watching her for the last fifteen years—I've seen what she does to her friends, never mind her enemies."

I don't want to keep up the dialogue with him. I don't like it. I let it go. Hayley's too much of a goddess to me. She's there, embedded in me, in a part of me, for too long. I don't know how to fix this. I don't know how to come at it. But I'm not going to bail. It's what I've hungered for, dreamt of, quietly craved, for too long. I just have to see how it falls. I *can't* push Emy away. And I *won't* give up on Hayley—I never will. I'm still stuffed. I'm still in raptures—I always will be. All the babe's got to do is sniff or yawn or beckon, and I'm there. I'm still bewitched. And he's her brother, so what does he know? It's like me warning some guy off my sister—what do I know? Heaps, but it doesn't count for anything.

We get a few more waves. I see Drewe on one as I'm paddling back out—he lays it flat down on the bottom turn and comes off the bottom in a long slingshot that fires him up into the wall as the feather of the lip begins to peel. And then he drags a casual hand, and fades back into the barrel. For an instant, he disappears, within that revolving, boring, white-blue perfection of water—does that quintessential thing that a surfer can do—*gets inside*. Then he re-emerges, poised for an instant, in a calm stance of grace—like a casual god. Then suddenly he explodes out of that, with a great flare of a cut-back that sends spray arcing way out over the water.

We give up the chat about the babes. It doesn't seem to be helping either of us. We stay out there as the fish start to jump—silver, snapping arching bodies in the dusk—leaping out of the darkening water ten foot from your board. And another surfer out there keeps going "hey" and "whoa" each time they jump 'cause it's such a buzz, and you pull your feet up out of the water, 'cause you don't know what's making them jump, you never know what's chasing them.

CHAPTER FOUR

WHEN I GET HOME DELIA'S HAVING DRINKS IN THE "parlor"—as she calls it—with a couple of her teabag mates. They're out to some show tonight or something or other. I duck for cover, skirt the grounds and slide out of view. They're always overdone dears with too much plaster on their mugs, too much metal hanging off them, and minds about as radical as an azalea bush. The old man's back down the yacht club, and not back yet.

I have a shower, and weather that Saturday night buzz that starts to rise in you—that slow whirr of anticipation and excitement that builds. After my shower I watch the box a bit out in the back room while I eat. I listen to the teabags cackle and carry on out in the parlor—and get ready to bolt out into the backyard and dive under a rose bush if I hear anyone coming. Big Sis went to tennis and isn't coming back till late. I reckon she's on with the tennis coach but I can't prove it. Wish I could—Delia would absolutely do her nut—it's law students, med students, dent heads, and nothing else. Tennis coaches are right off the map—unless of course they happen to have won a couple of majors or something. Delia jumps me when I let my guard drop, I'm gnawing on a cold lamb cutlet and engrossed in some guy getting washed down a river in France on the news and I don't even hear the telltale clang of metal as she approaches.

"Matthew—I want you to come and meet my guests."

Oh Christ, this is fatal. And I can't tank it—I want the car tonight. The deal has been made abundantly clear to me in the past: you want the wheels, you tow the line. You want to be a rebel without a pause—you can walk.

I follow Delia back into the living room where she and a couple of teabags are getting tanked on G-and-Ts. Don't know where all the blokes are—bet they're all down the club on the piss already. Maybe they're all gay divorcees—I'm not enquiring. I hang there and do my bit. I've learned the drill—be polite, tip your hat, and get the hell out of there before they start wanting to know the size of your jocks and why you haven't got a girlfriend.

"Ellen, Deirdre—this is my son Matthew. He's just finished his HSC and he's hanging around acting like a delinquent all summer until his results come out. Then depending on how he goes we'll either send him down a coalmine or off to Sydney University Law School . . ."

"Or I'll disappear up the coast and get a job at the Big Banana . . ."

They have a bit of a crow. They like that one.

"Yes, well, there's a bit of a risk of that too . . ." Delia says, and sneaks me her "don't push your luck, sonny" look. Delia's a funny bitch. She gets with the other teabags and she really cuts loose sometimes.

One of her pals hooks into me right away. "Well, the end of school, hey Matthew—how fantastic. Are you going away? My Camilla's gone to Nouméa for two weeks."

"Yeah? Sounds good. Any surf in Nouméa?"

"I'm not sure. But I think she's too busy chasing the wind-surfing instructors to care . . ."

Watch she doesn't get a dose, hey, some of those boys really get around. Course I don't say that. I just stand there and grin like a simpering idiot. What in Christ are you supposed to say when some teabag tells you her sex-starved daughter's chasing wang in Nouméa? Hope she gets a good fuck? Christ, I don't know. I'm just some kind of retard lately.

"You going away, Matt?" the other teabag asks, and I have to say she looks marginally different, she doesn't have quite the level of "overdoneness" that is par for the rest of Delia's usual crowd. The hair doesn't look like it's just been attacked by a swarm of bees, the clothes are half normal. In fact, on looking a little closer, I notice she's got a sort of quality about her, a sort of style—must be a last minute ring in, I conclude, or she came to the wrong house and no one's noticed yet. The other teabag wanders off for a refill.

"Yeah, maybe. Just up the coast with a few mates. We're trying to sort it out."

"That sounds interesting. And what about next year—do you know what you want to do yet?"

And yeah, there it is, the routine *Have you sorted out the rest of your life yet?* question. And yeah, I just about launch into the stock standard response—the *everything's hunky-dory and I'm off to uni bright-eyed and bushy-tailed* prattle—like I've trotted out probably half-a-dozen times in the last two weeks alone. But I don't, something makes me stall. I actually get this weird impression something different's going on here, like she's actually asking me something here and she wants to know the answer. It's the subtlest thing, something in the phrasing, in the way the words were spoken, in the look in her eye. It's like maybe, somehow incredibly, she's detected I'm not totally a hundred percent with where I'm going with my life. And I pick up on that and switch off the auto-response. And let a little of the way I've really been feeling lately rise in me. And besides, no matter how late it is in the piece, I feel I can't miss this opportunity to let Delia know a few things.

"Yeah, funny you say that," I say to her, " 'cause just lately I've been starting to feel like I haven't really got a clue. You know what I mean? I kind of thought I'd have things sorted out by now—but I still don't feel that sure about anything."

"Oh, don't be so silly, Matt—" Delia cuts in. She can't bear this. She turns to Ellen, "He's down for Arts Law or Law at Sydney—whichever he gets into . . . He's so clever—he could do anything he wants . . ."

But to watch, you wouldn't think Delia had even spoken. It's not that this teabag called Ellen is rude or anything, but she just doesn't seem to acknowledge what Delia said in any way. I don't know who this teabag is, but she's not the usual run of the mill. She just continues on with me, sort of like we're the only two there. "I remember feeling just the same, you know. My father was a district court judge, and he so wanted me to follow him into the law. I'd grown up never hearing about anything but the law, and it was like it had always just been taken for granted. But I finished school and I realized I really didn't know what I wanted to do. Just like you say it—I didn't seem to have a strong feeling about anything. All I knew was I didn't want to be a lawyer, and I didn't want to go off and have babies straight away and spend the rest of my days in domestic bliss in suburbia."

And that's it. She leaves it there.

But she's got me. And I lean into her space a little. "So what did you do?" I ask.

"I went overseas. I went to West Africa, and worked for the Red Cross as a volunteer . . ."

No shit. "Yeah?"

And I catch the expression on Delia's face, and it's not looking good. Underneath all that plaster that's holding everything in place she looks like she's about to have a stroke.

Delia can't hold back, she's got to go for the big save and get in here and straighten this one out, before this so-called pal of hers steers her son right off the edge of the planet. "And it was in West Africa, Matt, that Ellen decided she wanted to be a doctor—so she went off to England to study. Ellen's been a physician at the San for the last ten years, Matt."

Well, shit, I'm glad we sorted that out. I thought for a moment there she just camped out in the jungle for the rest of her days—smoking rolled banana leaves and swinging through the trees with the gorillas. I give Delia a big smile of relief.

"No, it wasn't when I was in West Africa, actually, it was later. We were in the Sudan, and there was this terrible local war going on—different warlords fighting and all these innocent people getting terribly hurt. That's when I finally decided I wanted to be a doctor—and so I went off to London to study."

No shit.

The phone rings. Deliaa looks positively pained. She almost looks for an instant like she's going to act like she can't hear it. She's got this look like she knows if she goes Ellen's going to whip out a hookah pipe and offer me a toke, and start telling me depraved tales of Tunisian nights. But the phone keeps ringing, and she says, "I guess I'll have to get that." Which is pretty fucking hilarious at the time. And off she goes.

"Your mother mentioned the problem you've been having with your feet, Matt," Ellen says.

"Yeah," I say. But wrong tack. I don't want to know about this. No matter how fascinating a bird this old teabag is, I'm still in therapy on this one. I tighten up like a bolt on the Harbor Bridge. It's not like I want to react this way, but it's like I can't seem to help it. It's just where I'm at. I've got this real sore spot about it all—I'm in total denial. If you're not my doctor, I just want to leave it out. I don't want to talk to anyone about it—not my mates, not any babes, not any old dears my old lady knows. I just want to get away and get it sorted by myself, and somehow get back to near as normal as I can. But she doesn't quit.

"Have you found out exactly what the problem is?" she asks.

"Yeah. They reckon the stuff like the cartilage is wearing a little. It's like an arthritis."

She gives a little nod that kind of surprises me with the understanding it seems to reflect. "I saw a little of that," she says, "when I was with the army. All that marching—not that surprising really . . ."

So what? Some other bastard's actually had this before me? She's got all the skills this one. She really knows how to hook you along. I ask in spite of myself, "So what? You were in the army?"

"I studied with the army in the UK. I had to, I didn't have any money—and I didn't want to ask my father for any. I was such a rebel." She laughs. "Oh, when you're young, you're so earnest. But we had such a fantastic time—we were all young and in London and running wild. It was the thing for young Australians to do back then—take off to England to find themselves. I ran into a bunch of young crazy Aussies who were finding themselves. It was the time of our lives." She sort of half smiles to herself, she's off with some recollection. "There's such a world out there, Matt. And it never stops. Your life can just keep happening, if you want it to."

Yeah, I guess so, I think. Yeah, that might be true.

"I went all over the place with the army," she goes on, " . . . and eventually I met my husband."

She pauses. Thinking back on it all, I guess.

"You must have seen some pretty amazing stuff," I say.

"I did. I saw some incredible things. And I saw some absolutely dreadful things—landmine injuries—there was an awful lot of that in some of the countries we were in. It's the most hideous business."

My mind kind of smacks cold up against the brick with amazement at that one. I can't believe my old lady's brought home a pal who's helped out natives in the West Congo and patched up landmine victims.

"That must have been pretty awful," I say.

"It is—people losing limbs—often children. It's the most dreadful business I've ever seen. I was with the UN for a while, we were doing everything we could against it."

I just hang there. I'm freaked.

"So have you found a doctor?" she asks.

"Ah, yeah, a guy over at Royal North Shore—he seems pretty good. Up to him I wasn't going so well."

"Well, that's good, particularly with your feet—they can be such tricky things."

"Yeah."

"Well, I'm glad to hear things are working out for you now. Your mother was getting a little worried. She said you seemed to be getting a little down."

"Yeah. Maybe a little. It was wearing me a bit. It seemed to be stuffing up my whole life."

She pauses. "Well, good luck. I hope it goes well. Your mother thinks so much of you, you know . . . she never stops talking about you up at the club."

She does fuckin' what?

But Delia's back. "That was your father. He asked can you fill the car up, please. He wants to go early tomorrow morning."

"Cool. No problem." I turn to Ellen. "I've got to get going— nice to have met you."

"He's taking a girl out."

But I jump on it, before it slides into the slop. "Nice to have met you," I say again. And it's funny to hear myself reciting those cant lines and actually meaning them. The irony doesn't escape me as I'm saying them. Then I'm gone. But I walk back down the hall to my room with a startling vision in my head, of landmine victims and foreign army hospitals and distant exotic places. With a sense of my place in the world altered. And with a strange only partly grasped sense of the worlds beyond the tidy brick houses and neat red roof tops that crowd to the shore along this quiet coast, beside a bright expansive sea. That is all I know.

* * *

I roll the car down the hill to Drewe and Hayley's place on the Fairlight shore. It's a big, square, pale rendered sort of place that runs to three floors as it covers the slope of the land on the foreshore. It's the best house I've ever known, with lots of big airy rooms, and lots of space. Down on the very bottom level there's sort of a games room that goes out through the French doors to the lawn that looks out on North Harbor. That bottom room has a pool table and a couple of ratty old sofas and a bar fridge that doesn't work and seagrass matting on the floor, and it's always sort of been the domain of Drewe and Hayley and their friends over the years. It was kind of allocated I think— their folks signing it over on the condition they kept their mates out of the rest of the house. And over the years we often hung out in the *wreck* room at Drewe's place—as we called it—never comprehending that when their old man said "wreck" he meant "rec." It was always one of those favorite places we'd head back to after a morning down the surf. We'd go back there and play pool and listen to music and play guitar or fix dings out on the grass and generally rave for hours about nothing or whatever. And it's been like that for years. And as we got older and the babes started to appear it only really changed a little. We'd still be raving and banging away at a guitar and listening to the latest album by whoever, but Drewe would also have his latest in tow and half the time he'd be off in some corner going for the endless-pash world record.

And pretty much always, Hayley was around. From the very

beginning when we were little farts carrying our pop-outs back around the Fairlight shore from a morning in the shore break at South Steyne. We'd head back to Drewe's and sit in the wreck room eating bowls of Weet-Bix, and Hayley'd be there, wandering in and out, giving us lip, running a commentary, telling us what a pack of dags we were—the girl had attitude from when she was four, I swear it. And she was always a stunner. And then, as it happens, we grew, and things changed. We got cars, and we got babes—or were supposed to anyway, if we had a clue—and Hayley was still always around. I'd hang out with Drewe, and she'd come and go. And we'd have little chats about this and that now and then. I think secretly I was always stuck on her.

Well, now she's fifteen. And I'm seventeen. And the only thing that's stopping Hayley Churchill from setting the world on fire is her old man. Old man Churchill is one strict bastard when it comes to Hayley. Up till now it's basically been *no parties*. Just *no*, full stop. She kept hassling, but he wouldn't budge. He wasn't a complete fascist though. She got around— she went to movies with her mates, she went to dinner, she went to shows and stuff in town and all that—just *no parties*— particularly no parties with that ratbag crowd from down the beach. The old man had a real *thing* about the surf culture. He was really down on it. He didn't like the hair, he didn't like the ratbag scruffy look, he didn't like the attitude. He didn't like the drugs and all the other shit that he knew was going around—he was really ugly on the whole lot of it. And because he'd surrendered a son to it, I think it made him even less inclined to lose a daughter to it. He didn't want his daughter associating *with that element.* He wanted her sailing and playing tennis and going to the movies with nice friends, not hanging out down the beach with a pack of surfie mongrels, or going to their wild parties and getting into God knows what type of shit. Until now, that had been the story—no parties, full stop—he'd always been real tough on Hayley. But that was only until now.

I knock on the door, and wait a bit, and no one comes, so I knock again. A southerly blew in late. Big and gray and blowy—filling the air with salt and bluster. A classic summer southerly, that way they seem to come at the end of a sweltering summer day. Two in the afternoon you're frying your brains out and it's over thirty. Seven-thirty at night the southerly's blown in and the temperature's dropped ten degrees and the night's all gray and blustery and coolish. The door opens and Hayley's there.

My heart kind of stalls. I kind of want to moan. She looks more exquisite than anything I ever dreamt. She's in this dark dress that's got no sleeves that's just so beautiful. And she's wearing high heels. And the dress and the heels just accentuate the tanned slim beauty of bare arms and her legs. And I feel like I've been hit, honestly. I can feel something inside me crumpling with the impact of her beauty. Something getting rolled over and crushed, it's just too much.

"Hi, Matt," she says, with just the littlest playful slowness, drags it out a bit, gives it the slightest lilt and sing-song like it's some sort of game.

"Hayley. How are you?"

"I'm great, Matt. Really great. Ready to go?"

"Yeah. God, you look fantastic."

"Why thank you. You have to come in." She turns. And walks down the hall for me to follow. "Mum and Dad want to see you. They want to give you the *look after our daughter* lecture."

I follow her. If she doesn't know the impact of the way she looks I'll eat my hat. The dress dips low on her back, and is just that little bit high on her legs. I follow her, thinking what an amazing, beautiful dress it is, the way it's this very dark brown that's almost black, and it has this dark pattern, this texture that is intertwined and beneath its darkness, and all I can do is watch the tops of her legs and her arse in the dress and her bare back and choke. She leads me into the living room and I think I'm still staring at her arse as I get there.

"Matthew, son, how are you!" Hayley's old man booms. He booms with everyone, but he particularly booms with young men who are surfies who are within ten foot of his daughter. He shakes hands with me. He has a hand the texture of lightly sanded wood, and it's so large and thick, you feel it enclose your hand. The bastard's probably known me for ten years now, but he's still giving me the *you're taking my daughter out* routine. "Sit down, have a drink before you go. What would you like—scotch, beer, a squash." It's not a question, it sounds like an order. It sounds like he's checking me out. I flick a look at Hayley, but she's on it before I even get to her.

"Dad, will you stop it! It's Matt! Christ, you've only seen him hanging around here since he was six years old. He's not a secret axe murderer, he's never had his license canceled or suspended, he's never been busted for stealing cars. Now can we get out of here! We're going to a party!"

Hayley's old lady appears. "Have a nice time, dear. Have a nice time, Matt."

Mrs. Churchill's always been pretty sweet with me. All she's ever wanted to do is feed me. "Thanks, Mrs. Churchill."

The old man's teetering a little. And I've gotten a sense of how things are changing. How Hayley's coming into her own.

The old man holds his hand out to me again. "Matt, take care. Have a good night, but take care. And have her home by twelve."

"Muuummm!"

"Ron. We've talked about this."

"One, at the absolute latest. No later than one, young lady."

"Fine. *One.* One is wonderful! All my friends get home at three or four, or whenever they like. But one is wonderful—one I can live with." Hayley takes my hand. Sort of snatches it out of the air. "Come on, Matt, you're taking me to a party, remember!"

Mrs. Churchill gives me a smile as I go. "Good night," I say.

"Take care, son," I hear Mr. Churchill say again, but I don't catch his face as Hayley spins me. She leads me down the hall.

Her hand is fine and slender in mine. I've never held it before. She lets it go as we reach the door.

We go outside and walk over to the car. Hayley's cursing and she looks like she could kick the ground. "God, they give me the shits. Why do I have to go through all this shit? I'm fifteen for Christ's sake. I've got friends who are getting pregnant!"

"Maybe that's why." I nearly clap my hand over my mouth as it comes out, but I miss it. *Shit*. And then I'm kicking myself. What a dumb-arse thing to say. She stands by the car door and looks at me just like that.

"Matt, don't be a jerk," she says.

"I didn't mean it like that."

"Really. Well how did you mean it?"

"I just meant—it's only normal for them to be worried about you."

"Oh really, well *whoopi doop*—have you got any other incredibly piercing observations you'd like to make?"

"Not right now."

"Good. Can we get in the car. I'm cold."

I open the door for her. She gets in. I have the feeling that everything has turned to shit in the space of about three seconds.

I go around my side and get in. Hayley's looking out through the windscreen with a preoccupied sort of look on her face. Sort of like I'm not there. Something kicks up in me. I guess I sort of figure I'll sort things out there and then.

"Hayley, why did you ask me to take you to Stink's party?"

She turns and looks at me. With this funny sort of look of wonder. Sort of like somehow she's only just noticed I'm there.

"Why, so I could get out of there, of course. Why else?"

She's looking at me. To sit and look in Hayley's eyes and be talked to like that by her is to feel yourself break up and come apart inside. You sit there in the beam, in the radiance of her beauty, and she's telling you you're not zip.

"Oh Matt, how can you be so stupid! We can never go out—you're almost like my brother. You're Drewe's best friend—and besides you're not my type."

It's my turn to gaze out through the windscreen like I'm alone in the world. I look at the southerly, rushing gray through the landscape, tearing the trees back and forth.

"Matt, you're such an idiot—honestly. Did you think?"

"I like you, Hayls."

"I like you too, Matty—but we can only ever be friends."

But we're not friends, I think. We're not even that. You wouldn't screw your friend over to get around your parents to get to a party, would you. You wouldn't use your friend. Or they're not really your friend.

I start the car. "I wish you hadn't used me."

"I didn't use you. I asked you if you'd take me to Stink's."

"And—?"

"And what? And you said yes."

"And it was the only way you could get around your old man to get to the party."

She laughs. "No it wasn't. I could have gone myself. Or

with Sheryl. He's cool now. I thought you wouldn't mind giving me a ride."

I listen to her, and drive. I feel like I've found some more out in life. I feel sad and learning. We swing around through the Lauderdale Ss and head into Manly.

"So when I was out the back with Drewe that time and you came out and said 'Will you take me to Stink's party?' all you were asking me for was a ride?"

"What else? Seriously, Matt?" She kind of spins a fair load of ridicule into her tone at the end.

We just drive for a bit.

Then she gets a bit of edge in her voice. "What is this, Matt? Sheila Watts called me up this afternoon and reckoned you had your tongue halfway down Emy Greene's throat down the beach this morning? Care to tell me about that? Planning to have a chicky babe on each arm tonight were we? *Yeah right*."

"She did that. I didn't do that."

She laughs. "God you're a hoot, Matthew Owen—'I just happened to be standing there and some chicky babe stuck her tongue down my throat—*honest, I don't even know how it happened.*' You've really got a nerve, Matt."

Boy, do I feel screwed all over. Boy, do I feel dumb. "I didn't mean it to happen. I was actually thinking about you."

She laughs. A long, delicious, sweet laugh, that I could love her for alone. "Oh, Matty, you're such a pearl. You were thinking of me. How nice. Well Matthew, I'm sorry, but I won't be thinking of you, because I'm not such a phoney. And I'm sorry if I led you astray."

We pull into the car park at Queenscliff. I park under the line of Norfolks that edge the reserve. Stink's party is in the old hall in the middle of the reserve. Across on the other side of the reserve is Queenscliff lagoon.

"You didn't lead me astray." I watch her in the half light. I'm awed by the fineness of her beauty again. "I was having myself on."

"Yeah, you were a little."

She hangs there a second. Studying me. And it occurs to me there is a quality of supreme sureness, of absolute confidence in her gaze. "You're a cute guy, Matt. Heaps of chicky babes are wild about you."

I just watch. I can't be bothered.

"Are you cool?" she says.

"Sure, I'm cool."

She leans over to me, and I get this whoosh, this rush, of her scent, her closeness, flowing upon me in the stillness of the inside of the car. She kisses me on the cheek. I feel the fullness, the softness of her lips. "Thanks for the ride, Matty. Don't wait up, hey . . . I'll get home . . ."

Then she turns, and flicks open the car door, and slides out into the creeping dark, and she's gone. Fine brown limbs, heady scent, that beautiful dress, into the dark.

I still sit there.

"Fuck."

I sit in the car. I can see the hall over in the middle of the reserve. See the guys I know rolling up with their drinks under their arms and their babes on their other arm. All clean and scrubbed and combed and pressed and fresh. It's the sweet end of the evening. Before everything gradually turns wild and dirty. Before the fights and the broken glass and the spew sprayed across the grass and the babes so pissed they're falling over and flashing their fannies at you. I've seen it all before. Too many times. I'm getting jaded and I haven't even done shit. My feet hurt, they just sort of ache. It's so weird—it's the fucking weather—whenever it changes suddenly my bloody feet hurt. I recognize the pattern of it now. I'm like an old man at seventeen.

"Well, *Matty*," I say to myself, "better get out there and enjoy it while you can." But still I sit there. "Sure," I say to myself.

I start the car instead.

CHAPTER FIVE

I DRIVE DOWN TO THE STEYNE. I DON'T KNOW exactly what it is that's got me in the guts, but I can't face it. I don't want to fucking know about it. Oh, that's bullshit—I know exactly what it is, and I just can't handle it. I thought I was taking Hayley Churchill to Stink's party, and it turns out I'm nothing. I'm a big zip. *How could you be so dumb?* I say to myself, as I drive along the beachfront. I park on the beach opposite the pub. The southerly's still blowing up a storm. Bit of swell tomorrow, I think, or maybe the next day. I walk over to the pub.

I don't know when I started drinking at the Steyne. But it's a crime whenever it was. I was doing Saturday nights down at the Steyne in Year Ten I know for a fact. I always just got dragged along by the rest of the crew—they got their licenses, they got cars, they hung out at the pub, I just cruised along with whatever. I've done my HSC, but I only turned seventeen a couple of months back. I'm the youngest guy in the crew. Stink, Lew, Spears, they're all older, Croc—he's nearly twenty—he's repeated twice.

The Steyne's been the hub of our set Saturday night routine for yonks now. It's kind of evolved over the years—we surf our arses off all day Saturday, we party all Saturday night. And no matter where the party's at or whatever's on—we always kick off and get primed at the Steyne. It's where you retreat to when the party you crashed's not happening. It's where you say "fuck it" and just stop back at when you've had enough of all the crap parties and crap dance spots some of the babes keep dragging us around to. It's where you can just hang back at and have a quiet one and piss on till you fade, when you don't want to know about where everyone else is heading. My old man runs a bit of a commentary on me and the booze—he's checked me out a few times after my *big* Saturday nights: "You won't be able to keep that up much longer," he says, "you don't stay bulletproof forever." Well, that may be, I think, but while I am bulletproof, I won't have to worry about it. Basically I can piss my brains out all Saturday night, and wake up not feeling a dent at five on Sunday morning—and away I go, for the early surf.

I buy a beer in the lounge, then walk out to the beer garden. I'm not expecting to find a soul. The plan is to get primed then work out whether I've got the balls to go back and face the ragging I'm going to cop 'cause Hayley gave me the flick. Gave me the flick—what? The babe never even took me on to give me the flick—she just sucked me in for a ride.

"Owl."

I look around. It's Poon. Sitting on a schooey at a table in the corner. He looks a bit undercover—he looks like secret agent X or something or other. He's kind of hiding out under the ivy that's hanging off the trellis overhead. "Whatcha' doin', mate? Why aren't you down at Stink's—what happened to the hot date?"

"Ah—never happened . . ."

He checks me out. "Leave it out, hey?"

"Yeah, let's leave it out, mate."

"Don't let it wear you, hey, mate—they're all pretty foxy . . ."

Pretty foxy—that's a start.

I sit down with him. I gaze at my beer. I check out the crowd. It occurs to me, incredibly, that I've probably drunk enough beer already in my life. I turn back to Poon. "So what's up? Why aren't you down at Stink's?"

"Plenty of time for that, mate—*I'm just waitin' for my man.*" Poon's doin' his best Joe-Cool-bad-head routine.

"Yeah." I try to be cool.

Poon's changed lately. I've seen it before. A year back he was cool—all he did was surf and hang out like the rest of us. Now, he's chasing some other trip—all he ever seems to do is try to score. I've watched guys in other crews head like that, slightly older guys that you've kind of seen around for years. They start to take on this manner, they get this wasted, distracted look. You don't see them out in the surf anymore, you only see them prowling the path or intently raving in some milko with some rabid-looking dealer type. You bump into them in the middle of the day and they're off their faces. That's where Poon's halfway to now. He's already in the cycle. Whenever you see him, he's either trying to buy, or trying to work out where to get wasted. There doesn't seem to be anything else anymore. And once he's scored, he disappears up the shop with Stink or Jewel or Hen or whoever else is *into it* and interested in a session, and they haggle about the price of the split, and buy an orange juice to make a bong out of the empty container.

But me. I'm still trying to be cool. "What you buying?"

"Just some ganga, mate. You want to have a smoke—" He cuts himself off, "*My man . . .*" He's up, "—mind my beer, hey man . . ." He does a beeline for some guy. I check the guy out, coming out of the door of the public into the beer garden—dope bag over his shoulder, semi-blond dreadlocks, big rasta tea-cozy cap. Fuck, all he needs is a sign hanging around his neck saying "I'm dealing."

I wait. I turn my beer glass on its mat. Draw a fingertip down its wet beaded surface. I drink and get that first slightly pungent, slightly sharp odor and taste of hops. I think to myself the first beer is always the best. It's just downhill from there. Poon and I have always been all right. A few years back when he was madder for the surf, we were closer. He did a few trips with Drewe and me up the coast—Soldiers, Crescent. We had great times. Poon was always a little quiet, maybe a little mucked about and unhappy at times. When he was younger I remember you always had this feeling he was just trying to survive things. His old man was an Aussie, and his old lady was Malay or Thai or something, I don't really even know. But they split up when Poon was fairly young and I think some pretty bad shit went on, and eventually things settled down and Poon lived with his old lady. But he always had it kind of tough. The old man would blow in now and then and give them all hell. Poon's clothes were always pretty shitty and you never saw him buying new wetsuits or boards or shit like that. The other guys in the crew would look after him—they'd sell him their boards for next to nix, sometimes they'd even give him their old wetsuits. Stink in particular was always really cool with Poon. I don't know why, but Stink was always looking out for Poon, giving him stuff. I always admired Stink for that. Stink came from a big house down on the water at Forty Baskets—swimming pool, tennis court, you name it—but Stink always still looked out for Poon.

I always remember the first time I saw Poon out in the surf—we used to call him Tiger back then. He was really dark, with long dead-straight black hair, and he rode a long fire-red diamond tail that he really thrashed around. I'd probably put him after Drewe to watch. He was all edge and charge and thrash—I think I learned how to attack a wave from Poon more than anyone else. It was more evident when you watched Poon what he was doing; you couldn't see things with Drewe, he had so much class, it was all kind of magical. But with Poon, I remember paddling out in a surf at Mid Steyne once and watching him take off on a long, long wall, thinking he'll never make that, not in a pink fit. And he just went at it, he just attacked it like you'd never believe, and he got so much speed, took such a fast line, it was like he flew along the wall—floating through sections, bottom turning around lips. I think of that, of the way Poon used to surf, and the way I used to watch him and how much I learned, and it actually pains me a little now, because lately he hardly gets out in the surf at all. And when he does, he just sort of cruises—all the muscle's gone. And he's really not out there much anymore, he shows late and all he's doing is looking to score.

"Faaark, man. Faaark, Owl. Top score. Top shit." Poon's back, grinning ear to ear. He sits down.

I drain my beer glass. "Want another?" I ask.

"Ah, fuck the piss, mate. Here, want this?" He offers his beer, "Yeah, knock that back, then we'll go have a smoke—then we'll blow into Stinky-boy's Barbie party."

I've never had a smoke. But right now I feel open to the idea of a smoke. "What's that?" I nod at his beer.

"It's New, mate."

"Can't stand the stuff. How about you finish that, and I'll go get a middy. Then we'll go have a smoke, okay?"

"Now you're talkin', Owl m'man." Poon's turnin' black, I swear. But I still like him. He's never been anything but straight with me. I've never seen him try to rip anyone off, or hurt anyone, or have a go at someone behind their back. He has a plain simple heart. He's one of those people, that amidst all the crap and sniping and other shit that goes on only ever seems to have a good heart. And sometimes you really can't help but stop and wonder how.

Poon sips his beer. I head for the bar. As I go I feel that first sweet rush that one drink gives you. That sweet, free-feeling giddiness. It probably doesn't get any better than that. From there we all only seek oblivion if we keep going.

"We'll go down on the sand, man."

"Down on the sand?"

"Yeah—behind the wall man, out of the wind."

"Yeah, cool," I say. I'll say *cool* to anything at the moment. I don't know. I don't care. Everything's cool. I'm just getting carried along. I bought another schooey instead of a middy back at the pub and as good as sculled it. The alcohol's hit perfect pitch inside, I couldn't give a shit about anything. If Poon says, "Let's sit in the middle of the Corso and whip out a bong," I'll probably say, "Yeah, cool."

We walk down the steps to the beach. I take my shoes off. "Yeah, take your treads off, Owl—feel the earth."

"—sand, Poon."

Poon's cacking himself. I think he's already ripped. Poon

hasn't got any shoes on. He hasn't worn shoes for a while now. It's this hippy trip he's on—he started going everywhere without any shoes in about the middle of winter and hasn't stopped. I swear, no matter how fuckin' cold it got in winter he was barefoot—I haven't seen him in shoes for months. Poon's heading seriously north. Another month or two and he'll be gone—living with some hill tribe back of Lismore, spending his days hugging trees.

We sit, our backs against the sandstone wall, in the dark, and Poon lights a joint. "Don't smoke it like a cigarette, Owl, you've got to hold the smoke in more—suck it down harder into your lungs and try and hang onto it a bit longer."

"Cool." I've smoked a cigarette. I feel a little relieved about that. If I hadn't smoked a few cigarettes along the way I'd be feeling critically uncool here. I take a long hard drag, it hits the back of my throat with a jab that sort of hurts and sort of doesn't—it seems to sort of carry its own anesthesia. I hold it down for as long as I can, then I let it go. "Faaark, it's the thickest smoke," I say between the splutters and the coughs.

"Yeah, good Afghani head," Poon drawls, "*faaark*—good ganga. Good gear, Owl man."

We sit, and feel it seep down into us—course down our spines, rise and move in a slow wave of color in our heads. Poon checks me out and reckons I'm a bit of a head for ganga. He says it just hits some people more than others. And he's not half wrong—I'm so spaced I'm ready to peel off from terra firma and drift into the ether.

I sit there, with my arse in the sand, my feet worked into the sand, which still has the last warmth of the day's heat, and just trip out—on the sound of the surf rolling out in the gray wind-torn night, on the mad rustling rush of the wind through every single thing, on the great gray spiraling night sky. I can't help it, but I keep saying to Poon, "Look at the stars between the wind, Poon. Look at the stars—they're so mad and moving tonight." And Poon's cacking himself, "You can't see the fuckin' stars, Owl man—they've put the roof on! You're the biggest fuckin' space cadet, man!" But I'm sure I can see the stars. And the thunder of the surf, rolling in the night out there, never stops freaking me. And there's something out there, a place I sense, a thing I know, an unknown that doesn't scare me. And my eyes search endlessly to find just what it is out there. But I can't see it. I never find it.

Then a little later, things start to pull back and calm and sharpen a little. Things start to seem slightly more normal again. I still feel warm and humming and strange, but the fizzing edge of perception has gone.

"The sand's warm, hey?" I push more sand up over my feet.

"Yeah. I know it mate," Poon says. "I sleep on the beach sometimes."

"Yeah?"

"Yeah. Get away from the racket. Old lady's got a new bloke. All they do is fuck each other's brains out—or slag each other to hell and back. Way it's always been with her—she can't pick a normal one she can just fuckin' get on a bit with—

it's always got to be fireworks one way or another. How are your olds, man?"

"Oh you know, the usual."

"Well this guy's a class A fuckwit. Follows me around hassling me about getting a job whenever he sees me. He's a builder—thinks that makes him God's gift to the fuckin' planet or something. He's not even my old man. Couple of weeks more—then I'm gone."

"Sounds like the go."

"It is, mate. When sleeping on the beach is better than sleeping in your own bed, you know it's time to split."

Poor fuckin' Poon, same old grief never letting up. It was like at school, half-a-dozen guys would be acting up and the teacher would come in and haul Poon out—he always seemed to be the guy that copped it. And it always seemed to me that they were taking the easiest target—like they knew he didn't have that invisible protection of his parents. Like it was apparent somehow he was uncared for. But shit like that just seemed to make his mates more loyal to him. Poon was the one guy in the crew every other guy would back up or stand up for without failure. Croc moved so fast on anyone that ever tried to hassle Poon they never even saw the truck coming. It was like all of us were conscious we'd had more and we were trying to make up to him for what he should have had.

"Got somewhere to go, mate?" I ask. "I'd offer, but I can't— I'm at home with my olds—"

"It's cool, Owl. I got a mate down in Moruya—I'm thinking of heading down there. Ricky Leare—remember him? Never surfed, but he was cool . . ."

"No. Was he at school?"

"Yeah, year ahead. Brown hair. Sort of stocky. Hung out with Bremmel and those guys . . ."

The *heads* a year ahead. The biggest pack of wasted characters you've ever seen. "No. Can't remember him."

We sit there.

"I've had a fucked life you know, Owl."

"Yeah."

"But you know what they say, hey, *It's never too late to have a happy childhood*. What a cack, hey." He laughs. "I'm workin' on having a happy childhood, mate."

I laugh too. I don't know why. But it seems fucking hilarious just then.

He stops. "Listen to the surf, hey mate."

We listen. Heads turned like a couple of wacked-out freaks. "Yeah."

"Fuckin' awesome, hey. I miss the surf, man. You're doin' the right thing, mate—never give it up. The other day I woke up, Owl, and I'd been dreaming of the surf. I was on this like long, long wall and I was just carving along it—looked like Nias or somewhere. And the funny thing was the way I was watching myself—I was sort of up in the air looking down on myself. Fuck it was weird . . . I got to get back out in the surf more, Owl—I keep telling myself that."

"Come down for the early tomorrow, mate. I get down at sunrise."

"You still doin' that crazy shit?"

"Shit yeah. Wouldn't do anything else."

"Yeah, sleep on the beach, and get up for the early," he says.

"Yeah. Do that."

We sit there with the big sound of the surf in the dark washing through our intoxicated heads. We just sit there and let it resonate in us. And the gray clouds of the southerly whip overhead in the dark. Then after a time that has the quiet and stillness of a short sleep, Poon speaks: "Let's go, hey man."

"Yeah, okay."

We walk back along the sand by the wall—it feels like velvet, between my toes, under my feet. And then back up the steps to the walkway.

"You coming down to Stink's?" I ask.

"Nah, maybe later, man. Want to go and see a mate . . ."

"Back to the Steyne?"

"Nah, place over on East Esplanade . . ."

Poon hangs there being buffeted by the southerly—wispy hair streaming about his face, bhagwan pants, embroidered vest, bare feet with anklet. He looks thinner. It's as if I see it for the first time, and it hits me all of a sudden how really wasted he's looking. Lew's really down on him lately, reckons he's becoming a real bad head. He gives him a bit of a hard time sometimes. Lew's a real drugs hardnose. Reckons you can piss it up with the Ra-Ra boys till you're brain damaged—but really gets down on anyone that's using anything else.

"Don't let these sorts get you down, hey Owl."

"Nah."

"They're not worth it. No offense to Drewe the Man—but his sister's a pain in the kisser—always has been I reckon."

Tell you what, everyone's got Hayley's number—everyone but this deaf, dumb and blind bastard standing here.

"There're some beautiful women out there, Owl—don't get stuck on a bad-news babe."

"Yeah."

"Like Stink's, Owl, too many Barbie babes. You can do heaps better than that, mate, they're nowhere." He shrugs. "Maybe I'll cruise down later—I'll see. Stink's always been such a cool guy—it's just his taste in women I don't like . . ."

I don't know why I say it, but I do. I kind of want to know, want to pry. Want to get a view into what he's getting up to, how he's living. "You going to score again?"

"Yeah, maybe . . . not sure . . . might just hang out . . . you know. It's just a place you can hang out . . ." He looks at me. And I get a sense of what's happening, to Poon, to all my friends, it's all falling apart. The last six years, the last eight years, all those surfs and parties and the good times, all that growing up together, it's all over, we're done. School's over and it's all falling apart, we're all growing up and out of it and going our own ways and it's all over. Poon's seen enough of Stink's parties to know he's not interested anymore.

He's about to split. I don't know why I bother to kid us both, but I do. It's probably the dumbest thing I say all night. "See you for the early, hey mate."

"Yeah, for the early, Owl," he bullshits back at me and we both know it's the biggest load of bullshit.

I step up closer to him. I feel all sad and lost and wasted. "Poon mate. Look after yourself, hey. You know what I mean."

"Yeah, cool Owl."

"Don't let bad shit get to you. Don't get fucked up 'cause it's been tough. Take care of yourself, hey. Poon, you remember in like Year Eight when like nearly the whole crew'd be out there for the early in the summer holidays and the light'd be beautiful and the water'd be so clear—you remember that?"

"Yeah, Owl. Those were good times." But he says it like they're gone.

We hang there.

"I'm thinkin' of goin' to Thailand, man."

"Yeah?"

"Yeah. Do a bit of a tour. And maybe on to India."

"*Yeah?*" I'm flipped out.

"Maybe in the new year. Maybe with a lady I know."

"You'll tell me, hey. You'll let me know. If you're really going to go."

"Yeah Owl, always. You and Drewe, man, I'd always tell."

He just hangs there again, wavering in the breeze. I feel a little lost and broken. I feel unsure about so many things. I feel sad and worried for him. I give him a hug.

"Take care, hey man," I say.

And we both stand there in the blustery air of the southerly saying *See ya, mate* and backing away to our different corners of the world. Then he's gone, down the Corso, and I feel sort of dry and spacey and strange, as I'm left on my own looking up the beach contemplating the distant void of Stink's party. I look at my watch and it's only a little after 9:30, and I freak out a little. It felt like about eleven. I was ready to go home. I try to remember where I parked the car. And it occurs to me sort of absentmindedly, amidst half-a-dozen other things, that Poon's probably going to buy smack.

CHAPTER SIX

I WALK NORTH, BACK UP THE BEACH, ALONG THE path—all the way back up to Queenscliff—buoyed and carried by the southerly at my back. I go by the Queensie Surf Club and under the bridge to get around to the reserve. Halfway through I realize there's a couple making out up against the wall under there—the full bit—she's got her dress up and he's got her up on the stone ledge that runs around under the bridge, and they're going at it hammer and tongs. I slide on by, quiet, but I suspect I could take a brass band through there and they wouldn't even notice.

As I cross the grass over to the old hall where the party is I sort of check out the whole scene as I approach. I'm feeling stone-cold sober. Which strikes me as being kind of cool. If I'd finally fronted up a pissed, blithering idiot it just would have made me a bigger, sillier bugger. The ganga has moved through me in a strange way. My emotions feel stripped and stark and uncluttered. The light's streaming out of the old hall and the music's thumping out, shaking the park, and as you get nearer there's people all over the place. People strewn over the wide concrete steps that run up to the big old wooden double doors, people all over the grass—hanging out, making out, rolling round, crashed out, pissing on, bonging on, you name it. I pass some chick having a fucking bitch fit—she looks like she's knocked back a bottle of Bundy or something all by herself and now she's doing the screaming spin-out—she'll be spewin' her guts up in half an hour. I don't recognize her, or any of her pals—they look a little young to me. It all looks like the usual shit—*gone beresk* as Hen likes to say. It looks like every dog and his sister's rolled up. I kind of like it like this, I'm thinking to myself as I go up the steps and inside. I kind of wanted to cruise in unnoticed, and I couldn't make a better job of it if I tried. The place is going fucking beserk and I'll be lucky if I get a hello. Maybe I'll just take a look around and piss off. *Hey guys, I tried, but it just didn't happen for me.*

I get inside and it's like the whole floor is flexing up and down. The dance lights are all blue and purple and red with some mad strobe light system going and there's just this sea of bodies moving up and down like a great tribal mass to the rhythm of the music, to the throb of the lights. I stop and hang at the door and watch it, it's the maddest scene. It looks like the end of the world; it looks like people gone out of their cones.

"Ooowwwll! You mad fuuuckeeen baaastaaad! Wheryaa-fuuckeeen beeen!"

It's Stink. Babe hooked under each arm, holding him up. He's got a bottle by the neck in each hand that's slung around them. He looks more than a little wasted—but fair enough—it's his party. The babes are looking a little worn—he's all over the place, it's probably breaking their backs trying to hold him up.

"Hey, Stink. Happy birthday," I yell above the stomping roar.

Stink smiles, then jerks in real close to me with his babes on either side. He's up real close, and I get hit in the face with the pungence of alcohol and smoke and sweat and cheap perfume and whatever else he's stuck his face in tonight.

"*Fuckin' stuck-up mole she is, mate*," he raves. "No wonder you fuckin' gave her the flick—total fuckin' slack mole. I'd piss her off too—wouldn't touch her with a fuckin' barge pole if you paid me, mate."

"Who?" I say, like I don't know, but I know straight off, like who else could he be raving about. I feel this sort of sick lurch in my guts. I kind of worry that Hayls is all right.

"That fuckin' mole you brought down here . . . I pissed her off, it's my party, I pissed her right fuckin' off. It's my fuckin' party . . ." He hangs there gazing at me. I realize how fully out of it Stink is. I don't know how the fuck he's even managing to stay vertical.

Stink says nothing more, and hangs there for an instant in front of me, sort of stunned, then he suddenly spins and plants his mouth up against one of the babes beside him and she complies wildly, and he just drops the other one who's sort of left there sullenly observing the two of them. Stink's got this babe's scrawny body sort of hard, he's sort of pulling her into him, and he's a big strong guy with a wiry frame, and she looks sort of enveloped like prey wrapped up by an octopus, and Stink's hand thrusts up her skirt and she looks like she's just loving it and they look like they're going to drop right there and do the horizontal cha-cha. Then Stink sort of puts her down and goes, "Come on, let's go fuck." And I flick a look to the other babe to check out how she's taking all this—and she's just giving them the most wicked eyeball. But Stink reaches out and grabs her hand just as he and the first babe are about to stumble away, and she goes sullenly tumbling after them.

Stink was screwing the art teacher in Year Eleven. He's carved the letters *cunni* on one of his thongs and *lingus* on the other. Oh yeah, that's the sort of smoothie with the sorts Stink is. And they just seem to lap it up. There's a procession of them endlessly following him around. And the big place his folks have down at the water at Forty Baskets—with the swimming pool and the tennis court, and the convertible BMW that's his old lady's that he cruises down the beach in now and then—doesn't hurt his stakes either. It all adds up. Like those two. I've never seen either of them before in my life, but nothing new about that. Stink turns up babes at a better rate than I buy

Tracks. I clear off. Stink's hard enough to talk to when he's straight. I don't want to risk him coming back.

I move around through the crowd. I don't know what the fuck I'm doing. I'm looking for Hayley of course. But I just don't want to admit that to myself. I see Drewe. He's dancing with some babe. I take a good look—it isn't Layla. I kind of go by, give him a nod, he breaks off and comes over. "Matt, where you been?"

"Ah, don't know." I ramble a little. "Went down to Manly— ran into Poon—had a smoke, had a rave . . ." I'm trying to be cool in case anyone's paying attention. Drewe *is* cool. He's so cool he doesn't even make a wanker of me by taking any of it up.

The babe's standing there. She's got the biggest, stupidest looking platforms on I've ever seen in my life. I reckon if she falls off 'em she'll do herself some sort of serious injury.

"Hey Lisa, this is Owl."

"Hi, Owl."

She's got that chemical blond sort of hair, and she's tall—or maybe it's just the platforms. Never seen her before either. You can tell Stink and Lew tee'd up the invites on this one. They've really got a talent. Drewe leans over and says something to Lisa, I can't catch it in all the racket. Then he turns back to me. "Let's get out of this for a bit, hey."

"Yeah sure."

We're by the bar. He leans through the crowd there and yells to someone—I catch a glimpse of Dills back there, and Drewe comes back with a couple of beers in one hand. He presses a long neck into my hand. "Bit warm, mate—all the cold stuff's gone. Shoulda fronted earlier."

I follow him outside.

"What happened with you and Hayls, mate?"

"Trashed it before we even got out the front door. We sort of had it out I guess."

We're standing at the top of the steps, over to one side by the railing. Watching the crowd, the scene on the grass. It's like one mad scene. There's people everywhere.

"What, as soon as you got down here?"

"On the way down in the car actually."

He grimaces. "Nice one. God, she's a piece of work. I don't care who else she runs around, but I wish she wouldn't muck about with my mates."

He seems really pissed. Even more pissed than just finding out that Hayls and I barely made it out of the house. "What's up?" I ask.

"Ah, she fuckin' blows in here acting like the wild thing and starts coming onto Stink and then they have some big fuckin' scene—I don't know what was fuckin' goin on, but I let Stink know I was around—but you know what he's like—if it's got a heartbeat he wants to wump it. Then she gets on the tequila and orange with her pals and they're all over the place, and last I saw she and Lew are going at it at a hundred miles an hour, and talking about going for a spin in the Porsche."

"Her and Lew?" *Wham!* You know that thing, where you

don't change on the outside, you hold it all in place, you hold it all up, but the bomb's gone off inside and it's demolished everything, you're the hollow man. Well, I do that. I stand there and cave in, and just manage to keep the facade up—*Hayls and Lew?* You couldn't turn the blade in me better if you tried. Sometimes I really can't stand the guy. He's really the only guy in the crew I really don't care for sometimes. I almost wonder for a moment, did she do it on purpose? And then I think no, Hayls doesn't care enough about how I feel to bother.

Drewe's watching me. "Fuckin' forget it, mate. I told you."

I'm still hanging there. Holding myself together. I can't think of anything to say.

"Think about it, Matt," Drewe says. "If Lew's the sort of guy she wants to get around with . . ."

"Yeah, cool," I say. But it's all still blown away and hollowed out inside. I'm fucked. I really am. It hurts. Lew—fuckin' believe that, it had to be Lew.

"Just fuckin' leave it, Matt. Just fuckin' forget it. There's no point."

"I will."

"Forget the bitch tonight. I'll keep an eye on her—she's my sister."

"Sweet."

"And next time you get stuck on a babe, make it a nicer one."

I hang there looking at my mate Drewe. I drink my warm beer. I'm thinking, it's not like that though, is it. It's not that clean and simple a formula. You get stuck on a babe, and she thinks you're a big zero and won't even say hello. And half the time some other babe starts following you around, and you don't want to know about her. If you can manage the whole arrangement—you like her, she likes you—then you've really made it big time. You've really scored.

Drewe's watching me. "She's a big girl, mate—you know that. If she wants to knock around with a suede head like Lew Castor that's her look out. They're fuckin' built for each other if you ask me."

"Cool. I'm past it, mate."

"Not over it, just past it, hey?"

"Yeah, something like that I guess. That'll do." I don't know what I want to do. But I don't want to talk about it anymore. My first attempt at getting a babe out has been about as disastrous as they come.

I say that to Drewe. I laugh. "Think about it. First time out. She tells me to piss off in the car, and pisses off with some other guy. What a nass." I start laughing, start cacking myself. It's pathetic. Drewe's laughing too. We're both there in stitches for a while, cacking ourselves at my first big hot date, sloshing our warm beer all over the place. What a *legend*. Wonder if I'll manage to get laid before I'm twenty-five. Faaark, talk about a hopeless case. I turn, and lean against the railing, and drink my warm beer. It tastes all right. Goes with the warm, blowy night.

We watch the antics.

"Check out this sort," Drewe says, pointing with the neck of his beer, out into the darkness. "Some grom's just fuckin' stolen her undies."

It's true, there's some guy bolting and hooting around the grass waving a pair of knickers. "Hey, that's Chicka."

"That'd be right—probably eat them."

I grin. I can't help but grin to watch it. If you didn't grin you'd be worried. It's the usual mad scene.

"Few bods, hey," Drewe says.

"Yeah, big roll up."

"Knew it would be. Cops have been through once already. Confiscated Ally's bong. And once a few of the locals check out that couple doing a sixty-niner over there on the grass I reckon they'll be back pretty soon again too."

I look over where he's looking. I don't know if he's having me on or not. "I can't tell what's fucking going on."

"Take my word for it, mate."

He hangs back against the hall wall. He looks knackered.

"Who was the babe?" I say.

"Some sort. Leapt off the smorgasbord in there at me."

"Like that, hey? Sounds tough."

"Yeah. And fuckin' Lewie's got to go after my sister."

"Who went after who, mate?"

"Yeah—fair point. It looked about an equal attraction to be honest. It's kind of depressing though—guess it gives me an idea how my sister's going to turn out. She's just not your speed—no offense, mate."

108   PAUL HAYDEN

"None taken." But something's taken. What is it? I was smitten with her, I'm still smitten with her, and it seems obvious to about anyone but me that I'm not her type—Lew Castor's her type.

"You seen them round?"

"Yeah, I'm sort of keepin' an eye on things. She's keeping her party dress on."

It's sort of hard to explain the dynamics of the crew to you, but Drewe's the only guy that could really say with any cred that he's keeping an eye on Lew. Over the years, if Lew was the leader of the pack, and he was, Drewe was something else again, he sort of stood apart, he was the nass, he was the guru. People were just in awe from a distance. He had more sponsorships than anyone on the beach. He'd won more contests than anyone on the beach—and half the time he didn't even bother to show to contests. Out in the water he had this aggression, this power, that was astounding. It was awesome. And it equated back through onto the beach. Drewe'd get in close and straighten someone out if he had to, he wasn't shy of doing the heavy. They sort of co-existed Lew and Drewe in the crew. Lew was the gang leader, and Drewe was the maestro. Lew wouldn't have had a moment's doubt that Drewe would front up to him if he had to.

"I need another drink, mate," Drewe says. He tilts his empty bottle at me. "You on for one?"

"Yeah. Guess so. I was thinking of pissing off."

"Yeah? You got to roll with it, mate. Sometimes you just

draw a blank. It's just like catching waves. You got to just keep going at it."

"Surf philosophers. Fuckin' marvel aren't they."

He grins. But he doesn't move off the wall for his beer. He's still hanging there.

I sit up on the railing, back to the mob, and check him out. "Where's Layla?"

"Who knows. Not answering calls. She's gone weird chick on me. Mate, things can change so fast. Tried to call her this afternoon—twice, this evening—twice, no answer. Think she pulled the plug. It's not looking good, mate."

"What's not?"

"Any of it. I've been thinking about it more, you know. I know I want to keep it now. I want to have it. It's my child. Even if she doesn't want it. I still want to have it. It's my child—my son, my daughter—whatever. I've been thinking about it, mate. I can't live with the thought. It's not an accident. It's your life."

"Yeah?" And that's just like Drewe. He's always been like that, sort of out there in his own world, seeing things his own way. Discovering what he's feeling and thinking and following it. It totally blows me away when he says that, but on the other hand, it doesn't surprise me at all. "So what's she say?"

"She doesn't say. She's not answering the phone, like I said. I'm planning on going around tomorrow."

"Yeah. What are you going to say?"

"What I just said to you. I've thought about it a lot and I

want to keep the baby. I don't want her to have an abortion. I know what's going to happen, she's going to think I'm nuts."

I hang there and think about it. "Is an abortion on the cards?"

"Course it's on the fuckin' cards. Yeah, it's on the cards. She's already mentioned it. Matt, the babe doesn't want to be a mum. She wants to be a friggin' supreme court judge far as I can work out. And this has gotten heavily in the way of it."

"Fuck, you can pick 'em mate."

"Yeah—and who's talking."

I almost crack a grin.

"So what do you do if she says no?"

"I'm fucked, I guess. I don't know. I'm trying to work it out. You tell me. What can I do if I say 'Let's have it—I'll look after it' and she says 'No—fuck off'? That's it. It's not like I'm going to take her to court or something."

"Shit—I don't know. This is unreal. You're only eighteen. What are you fucking going to do if she dumps it on your doorstep and goes 'Cool—it's yours, I'll be round first Sunday of every month to say hello'?"

"I don't fucking know. I'll live with it. But I've been thinking about this a lot. It's not like I just snapped my fingers and said 'Yeah, let's do it.' This means heaps to me, Matt. This fucking means something."

"Yeah?" And I can see it. But I kind of can't. It's so out there and far from where I am at the moment I can't quite get my head around it. "I don't know what I'd do, mate. If I got a babe pregnant and then she said to me she didn't want to keep it, I don't know what I'd do right now. I don't know that I'd fight it."

"That's cool, mate, I understand that. But I'll tell you it's different when you're there, when it's happening to you. Look at your old man, mate, and then think that's what you are to this—you're the father and it's the child. Think of that. It's not the same until it happens to you, mate, it's nothing like it. I was pretty much like you until this. The first day she told me, I just sort of went, yeah, all right, no sweat, probably having herself on, maybe have an abortion right, maybe miscarry, no big deal. But it is a big deal. It's just kept growing in me. I just kept thinking about it and I couldn't let it go. It's not a little thing, it's bigger than anything. It's life. That sort of dawned on me the other day."

"Yeah, but what about the babe—Layla Honso? What about that?"

"I know—I know. I don't fucking know. I screwed her didn't I. It's my lookout. I should have thought about that."

"It's not your fault, mate—she told you she was on the pill."

"She *was* on the pill, mate—she wasn't trying one on. Layla was just out for a bit of a good time till she got to law school where she could suss out the judges' sons and nail one down. Mate, it couldn't have happened weirder. Mate, I've screwed babes and we haven't even discussed who's using what, we've just got it on. Layla—she's always raving about it, she's the most neurotic sort I've ever met. It's unbelievable."

We hang there. And think about all that. Off in the distance there's a siren. I follow its willowy trail carried on the salt breeze. It's not coming nearer. It's drawing away.

"Well, you've got me stuffed," I say. "I haven't got a clue what you should do. I can believe it—but I can't believe it. I can understand why you would want to do it. But it doesn't mean it isn't fuckin' wild. You told your olds? You told anyone else?"

He hesitates. He draws breath and gazes off into the murky light of the park. Barks and hoots of mad times carry back from out there before he speaks. "Yeah—I told my old lady."

"What did she say?"

"She said to follow my conscience."

"No shit."

"Yeah. No shit."

"That's all?"

"Yeah. That's all. She said I was an adult now and it's my scene."

"Yeah. Well it's true isn't it. School's over. It's all over. It's like it's all busting up—all of this. You can't kind of stop it."

Drewe just nods. He looks down. "It's fucking heavy duty, mate, I'll tell you that. It's wearing me. Let's go get another beer."

"Yeah. Let's get a beer. Even if it is fucking warm."

But Hayley and Lew come up the steps right then. Arm in arm. Close. Pulled together. That way couples walk when they really feel something for each other. Like they're joined at the fucking hip or something. I swear, it's like a punch in the guts.

I swear, I nearly double over. I just go clam, I feel like I can't draw a breath. You wouldn't think it could cause you so much pain just to see a person with another person. But it was all vested right there. I was so stuck, so infatuated, so absolutely ga-ga over her, it doesn't just fade like you turned the telly off. I see her and my whole world lurches.

"*Whoo-hoo!*" Hayley hoots. "Matty, Drewe, you should have seen the spin we just went for! Whoo-hoo! The Bilgola Ss with the top down—oh God, what a blast! And it's such an unreal night!"

Lew just hangs there gleaming like Mister Unreal, with Hayley on his arm. You want to kill the bastard. Mister Unreal's got Hayley. I swear I could do it, I could drive a stake through his heart. I get this pang of feeling like the greatest loser of all time.

"You guys for real—Bilgola? What were you doin' all the friggin' way up there?" Drewe says.

"Hayley wanted to check out the car—then she wanted to drive—"

"You fuckin' drove? Are you nuts?"

"Not through the Ss—in the Warriewood car park."

"And it was so grouse," Hayley coos. "That car is so awesome. It just throbs—"

We all stand there. I feel like someone just smacked something—a dream, a hope, a wish—some essence of my whole world, over the head with a cricket bat. The pretense, the desire, the illusion, is all gone. Hayley reckons the car throbs, and Mister Unreal's got his arm tight around her waist in that way that when you hold a babe it feels so good. And I swear I'm standing there holding myself like cracked plaster and trying to hold back the pain behind my eyes.

"Take it easy, hey guys," Drewe says, "don't do anything dumb."

"Oh big brother, will you piss off. Lewis is looking after me."

"It's cool," says Lew, "I've had one beer. That's it."

It's true. Mister Unreal hardly ever drinks. He just captains the water polo team, plays for the Manly Ra-Ra colts, and drives his old man's Porsche—or whatever other bit of hot-throb machinery happens to be lying around the old man's workshop, and screws the prettiest babes. The bastard barely drinks at all—doesn't get the time—you'd never see him staggering around like a smashed lost cause late on Saturday night. The bastard's just too plain suave—he's either rubbing up against some velvet babe or discussing what's under the bonnet of what's out front with some other suave. Beats the fuck out of me how it is he surfs so average.

I glance at Hayley. I catch her in an instant when she's looking back at me, and I catch something in her eyes, something maybe you could mistake for recognition of something else that happened, for acknowledgment of having caused hurt, and perhaps a little regret—but then it's gone, and the silken veil goes back up over her eyes. And she looks away. And it's like it never happened. I stop looking at her.

"Catch ya, guys," Lew says. "Top party, hey." Lew tugs

Hayley along with him by the waist. Toward the door. And they're gone.

I hang there. Thinking about it. Hanging there on the landing railing like a boxer on the ropes who's just copped one in the guts, and it's a real goodie that's going to leave him stuffed for a year.

Even the thing with Lew's bullshit. I've got no real bone with him, never have had. We've always just gotten on and done our own thing. We've never been at each other's throats. The guy's never tried to give me a hard time in my life. I just can't hack it—he's Mister Unreal, and I'm not. I don't seem to know where the fuck I'm at. And Lew is one of those guys that seems to know exactly where he's at every fucking minute of the day. What he wants, what he wants next, what he's going to do, and exactly how to get it all. Kind of like Hayley, I guess. That thought occurs to me just then, another punch in the guts.

They've gone inside. I don't want to go back inside anymore. I don't think I could bear it. If the babe wants to set me up and give me the flick, cool. But I'll be fucked if I'm going to hang around all night watching her rub up against Mister Unreal. I just hang there. I can't bear to move.

"Chin up, mate."

"Yeah, sure. I'm pissing off. I've had this."

"May be the move."

"I'm not hanging round, mate. I can't bear it."

"Cool. I can see it. Me too maybe. This stuff with Layla's driving me around the twist." Just as he says that the blond with the big platforms comes romping out through the doors, "Drewey!"

"Babe!"

She doesn't look as hot under the scrutiny of the white lights above the door.

"Aren't you coming back inside? Aren't we going to dance some more?"

"Sorry babe, got to split. Just got a call from the missus—the kid's giving her hell."

Fuck he's a hoot. This sort nearly falls forward off her platforms.

She looks at me. I do my best goddam shrug—I swear it's a beauty—it's like don't ask me how many kids he's got at home.

She turns, and can't bolt fast enough back inside to the mob.

We both crack up. We're in total fucking stitches.

After I recover I say, "Mate, are you for real? What are you fucking doing?"

"No idea. Thought I'd just try it on. I've been thinking I'd better stop going around poking my dick in mutton till I get this business sorted out."

"Oh, very eloquent, mate."

"Yeah—like it . . ."

Dills comes out of the hall with his babe on one arm and a long neck locked between each finger of the other hand. He sees us and veers over toward us and swings the hand loaded with beer up to us, offering, without saying a word. Drewe takes one. I shake my head, but give him a nod of thanks. I'm sick of the piss. Dills tumbles down the steps with his babe and the remainder of his beer bottles without a word.

Drewe twists the top off. "Dills, my man!" he hollers, in the direction of Dills' back that is melting into the crowd on the grass. Dills shoots an arm up punching the air in reply, without a sound or a backward look.

Drewe takes a long swig. Then leans back. "Life's happening, mate."

"Fuck yeah," I say. "And how." And no matter how much "it happens" it's pretty much always a self-centered universe, it occurs to me. Drewe says life's happening—but I'm not really thinking about unexpected babies. I'm thinking about how Hayls did me over and where it's going to leave me. I'm wondering about my feet and the op, and how it'll end up. I'm thinking about the way my world keeps changing, and how you never see stuff coming. You never dream of it. Then the next minute you're in it, and you just can't believe it. It's just happening and you've got to deal with it.

"You know what I was thinking about today, mate?" Drewe says. "I was thinking about in Year Seven how we used to meet in the morning for the early just when the lights went out and we started that thing with the cigars."

"Shit we were nuts. What the hell were we on about?"

"Fucked if I know. I started knocking off the old man's cigars—'cause I could, I guess. Then we kinda figured it'd be a good idea to have a smoke before we went for our sunrise surf. Hah! What a couple of headcases."

"But it was fucking great, remember."

"Yeah, mate. It was the best."

We both hoot with the past madness of it.

"You know the thing when you're a kid, mate, you're fucking cast iron. You're fucking indestructible. How would you fucking be—we rock up down the surf in the middle of winter, still fucking dark, sit and smoke a cigar and eat a chicken sandwich, then go for a winter surf. Who else but kids could be so loco?"

"My old lady made a mean chicken sandwich, didn't she."

"Too right—heaps of mayo." He sighs. "You're right, mate, it's all over . . . No more cigars at sunrise."

He takes another swig from his long neck. He looks at me. "So what's happening, mate?"

"Nothing. I'm pissing off."

"You've been pissing off for the last two hours."

"I'm still pissing off."

He leans forward and offers the long neck. I take it, and take a swig, and pass it back. "Christ—it's cold. How'd they manage that?"

"Must be Dills' special stock—*for the heavies*—"

For the "heavies" yeah, I think. "Remember when we wanted to be 'heavies'?" I say. "Remember when we used to surf South Steyne pipe and hang on the beach checking out some big dude taking off on a big North Steyne set and we thought that was absolutely it—we thought that was absolutely the top of the pile—and we'd be wondering, *How the hell do you make it all the way up there?*"

Drewe thinks. Bottle poised at his lips. "Just happens without you ever noticing it, doesn't it. You just grow into it. It's been a long time since I saw a wave at North Steyne that I wasn't game to give a shake."

"Time you went OS, mate—Indo, Hawaii—you've got to keep progressing. You're post North Steyne heavy now, mate—it's all over."

"Yeah, well, it may be well and truly all over."

We hang there.

"What about art school?" I say.

"I don't know. Maybe put it back a year. Maybe it'll never happen. Maybe I'll get a job shaping for Snapper—he keeps asking me. Or maybe I'll mix concrete for the old man."

"Ah, mate, that's not what you want. You've said as long as I've known you that's the last thing you ever want to do . . ."

"Things have changed—I've changed."

"Are you for real?"

"Yeah, Owl, I've changed. I'm just being honest. It's making something. It's building something. I did the weirdest thing the other day. I stopped outside a building site in the street—and I just stood there, watching the bastards. And I was thinking, they dig a great big hole, then they fill it up; they make something, they see it through to completion. I know you think I'm having you on, but it's for real. I was even thinking about architecture."

"Christ, you're freaking me out. Would you shut up."

"Why?"

" 'Cause I don't know what the hell I'm doing. I don't even know what the hell I want to do. It's not like I want to lie on the beach all day—but I just don't seem to have a fuckin' clue what I'm going to do . . ."

"Olds still want you to do Law?"

"Are you fuckin' kidding—my old lady's already bought me the bloody gown and wig."

He laughs. "That'd be right . . ."

"You said it."

"What about the old man?"

"He wants me to do *something*. He doesn't want me to do nothing. And he thinks an Arts degree's too close to nothing to be worth a frig . . ."

"Is that what you want to do? An Arts degree?"

"That's the only thing that sort of interests me—"

But Drewe cuts me off. He's come forward off the wall and he's leaning out over the railing, peering intently out over the crowd on the grass. "Oh fuck—is that Croc?"

I turn and look.

Over at the edge of the park under the trees there's some guy quite openly going hammer and tongs into some babe up on the bonnet of a car. He's got her arse up on the bonnet and all you can see is the bright white band of his rear as he goes at it and his jeans slide down, and the brown M of the babe's legs.

"Nah, he'd have her up in the tree if it was Croc . . ."

"See ya, guys!" someone calls from the other side of us. We turn, and it's Hayley and Lew going by. "Catch ya later." They don't stop. They parade by, arm in arm, down the steps, and they're gone. It's like for a second everything's coming at me from all sides. There's some mad head bonkin' some babe over on the bonnet of a car over there, and Hayley is cruising merrily by again, kicking me in the ribs.

I watch them go. Away. Through the mess of people. Hayley looks so happy. She's raving dizzily, all lit up. She's all chirpy and hyper, like she's had a few more drinks. Her beautiful brown dress has ridden up her arse a little and her legs look stunning. I forget the gorilla under the tree. Probably is Croc. Croc and his Bucket, as he likes to call her. Couple of months back they got it on at a party halfway up a set of stairs. People had to climb over them to get to the dunny. But I don't look back at Hayley. I couldn't care. I don't look at anything.

Drewe half grins to himself. He's watching Lew and Hayls disappear across the park. "Lovely sort. Glad I'm only related to her." He looks at me. "What's up, mate? Close-ups too rough?"

"Yeah."

"Fixed up all your illusions, have we? Thought she was so sweet and peachy, did we?—it was making me puke."

"Guess I know better now."

"And how. So what's happening, mate?"

"Nothing. Everything's fucked. I'm heading home." I swing forward off the railing. I gaze around. "I'm actually getting sick of this shit, you know, mate. Like how many of these do you think I've been to over the last few years. And they're always the bloody same. I'm feeling old, mate. I'm looking at some of this crowd and thinking they look like fucking kids."

"Fuck you're going to be a fun bastard when you're eighty, mate." Drewe laughs.

I grin.

"What's your problem, Matt? Make it happen. Go chase some talent, mate. You can't wait for them to come to you—that's your problem, mate—you've got to go after them. That's the way they like it—no matter how much of a spunk they think you are."

"Thanks for the pearls, bro."

"No sweat, bud."

He comes off the wall. "I'm headin' back inside. Another warm one, then I'm out of here. What are you up to?"

"I'm cruising home."

"Down for the early?"

"Yeah, mate."

"Reckon this southerly's going to make it happen?"

"Might."

"Catch you then?"

"You on?"

"Fucken A, mate—my days are numbered—I've got to make the most of them. I'm going to be changing nappies instead of waxing my stick at six in the morning soon." He stands in the doorway and checks me out. "Listen mate, why don't you just forget the bitch and get your act together and get in here—it's a regular smorgasbord—"

"Forget it. Some other time. I couldn't pull a babe tonight if I threw a rope around her."

Drewe heads back through the door. The music's thumping out past him, washing around him and onto me, like a wave surging by. "Check ya, Matt—for the early."

And as he turns his back and goes it occurs to me that Drewe's the coolest bastard that's ever lived, because he's always treated me like just the most normal Joe. He's never once backed up and gone, "Hey Owen, I reckon you're totally fuckin' weird. I reckon you're the weirdest most useless bastard that ever lived." When the fact is, I've never quite been the most normal Joe. I've always been off on my own trip somehow. I've always stood apart from the crowd and sort of done things in my own way. And through that, he's never said, "Matt, you're pretty fuckin' skewed." It's like this shit with Hayley. It's like this shit with my feet. It could only happen to me. I swear, I think I've never been normal. And, thing is, Drewe's always been the local legend—always the guy all the other guys were copying, the guy all the babes were out of their heads about. And even with that, we've always been the best mates, he's always been so cool, and never once looked at me and said, "Owl, you're from a different planet."

I stay there for a moment longer, looking out on the mad landscape of the party. And I have a vague thought about Emy. My eyes search for a quiet instant I deny within. I wonder where she might be. Is she here? Did she show? I keep scanning for an instant longer. Telling myself I'm not really looking. I'm not really hoping. I don't really care. Telling myself I deserve nothing. Because I know I do. Confronting just then, whether I like it or not, some place in my heart. Some point where my selfishness collides with my naiveté. It occurs to me, just then, no matter how much I don't want to admit it, I'm just like Hayley—only out for what I want. Only after what I desire. I have no right to think about Emy now. I have received everything I deserved. I'm just like Hayley—pursuing, indifferent, casual to the feelings of others. As callous as only a heart that *wants* can be.

Then I feel the last of it quit in me. And I go down the steps and just wander away. The thing with Hayls really hooks into me then. All I want to do is retreat. There's just no life, no urge, no desire left in me. I never gave a stuff about Stink's eighteenth—I only gave a stuff about Hayls. I was taking Hayls somewhere, I was going to be with Hayls. As I walk, I recall I left the car down at South Steyne. I cross the park and the road, and go back over to the walkway along the beach. I don't know that I've ever felt so bad. It's that thing, where reality, where what really happens, crashes into expectation, anticipation— rolls right over it and trashes it. I can't believe it got trashed so bad. I can't believe I was so hung up on Hayls and I just got it so fuckin' wrong.

I cross the grass over to the beachfront. The wind's in my face—the southerly. It's just steady now, thick, damp, solid—a big wind that can blow for days and days sometimes. I wonder how long it will last, I wonder when it will give out. Just as I get to the North Steyne club house a car goes by up the beach toward Manly, some sort of red sports number really scream-ing up North Steyne, thrashing the gears, engine screaming. It rockets by. Someone screams from it. Almost like they're screaming at me. I sort of catch it and I don't, 'cause I'm kind of looking the wrong way—I'm looking out at the dark blue muddiness in the direction of the ocean and sort of ignoring the din of the car as it's first approaching 'cause it's just anoth-er dumb-fuck hoon. And then when I turn it's kind of a little too late and it's pretty much rocketed by. I keep walking, and it's not till I get up toward Mid Steyne that it occurs to me that the Porsche Lew tears around in sometimes that is his old man's is red. And I wonder if it was Hayls and Lew.

A minute or two later two cop cars go by going the other way. Cruising low and quick that way the cops do—nose down, no lights on, one car close on the tail of the other. They're heading back down the way I just came. I reckon they're on for another roll-up at Stink's. The cops love the surf scene, all that juvenile drugs and sex and rock'n'roll—whips 'em into an absolute frenzy. I reckon I know three-quarters of the Manly station by sight. They're always around. One time, middle of winter, freezing cold, the surf's stuffed, whole lot of us barreled over the road to an abandoned block of flats right on the beach the developers were about to pull down, just to get out of the weather for a bit. Half an hour later three squad cars pull up—two out the front, one out in the back lane—had a tip-off some *major crime* was going on. Fuck it was a hoot—

they rounded the whole lot of us up and ferried us back to Manly station for the big line-up—and in the end all Sergeant Porky could do was give us all the big lecture on getting a haircut. Sometimes the pigs just haven't got a clue—there's dickheads selling smack to twelve-year-olds in the North Steyne dunnies, and they're staking out the beach nabbing ten-year-olds knockin' off coins from someone's jeans.

I find the car and cruise home. Through the quiet back streets of Manly, and up the dark hill to Fairlight. I reckon if I get any duller I'm going to fade away. But I can't help but wonder how I managed to screw so much expectation into the ground. I pray for a wave tomorrow. So I can get out there and get buried in water and forget. I pray for a big southerly swell that shakes your bones and makes your heart thump and blows all the crap away. I drift into sleep with a vision of Hayley in her dark brown dress and she says something nice to me in my dream, something that's sweet and caring in a soft clear voice, but still I can't quite make it out, I can't quite make the words out . . .

CHAPTER SEVEN

IN THE MORNING MY FEET HAVE REALLY PACKED up for some dumb reason. They're stiff and sore—I wake up early with the hurt of them. I creep out of bed and wander out to the balcony in the half light to check out the weather. It's all gray and blowy. There's a light drizzle, and it's turned on-shore from the southeast. "Don't bother," I say to myself, "everywhere'll be fucked." I creep back to bed. And creep is the word—my feet are really playing up. I don't know what sets them off—maybe it's the booze, maybe it's the weather, but I'm past trying to pick it. All I want now is just to get on and have the op and get it sorted. I'm seeing the doc again on Friday—and I'm looking forward to it. I'm sick of riding the ups and downs. I crash back into bed. I start thinking about

Hayley and last night. And I lie there, sinking back into the murky morning light, and I feel like I could cry. I wonder how you can be seventeen and everything can be so fucked. But that doesn't help it or change it. I just lie there sinking into it, and I fall asleep again.

I sit the whole day out. I do next to nix. When I wake up again it's almost eleven. The olds have left me a note—they've gone to some do down at the yacht club all day, and Sis is out for the day with her uni pals. That's all okay with me. I could use a little space. I hang on the sofa and read yesterday's papers and watch the sport shows. One show has a piece on an American gridiron legend who's done his knee. The guy's gone from national icon to worker in a rehab center in about the space of a year. And that's kinda what it's all about—how this guy's sorted himself out by his own means, by going off to work in this rehab center for victims of major accidents—like car crashes and industrial accidents and stuff like that. It's all so all-American hunky dory the syrup is pretty much just running off it. But the guy's cool. He's not a put-on at all. You can see he's just one of those big savvy sweet-natured hard-playing guys. He talks about how he grew up living and breathing football—then he made the major leagues—and he's the hometown dream come true. Then he gets done in a big two-way tackle and blows up one of his knees 'cause it gets rotated—and it's all over in the twinkle of an eye. It's just fuckin' tragic. And I keep wanting to change the channel away from it, 'cause I'm just waiting for the bastard to start thanking Jesus or what the fuck. But I can't, the piece sort of holds me in a way I don't want to admit. I watch it through to the end. I reckon the guy's got more grace in his left elbow than I could summon in a lifetime. The last scene is him coaching a little league team and talking about how you've just got to get on with your life. Bastard makes it all sound so cruisey you've got to wonder what he's on. I switch the box off for a bit after it finishes—like I can't hack anymore just for the minute, and I find myself wishing I could just take away a little something from it. Just a little sliver of grace I could call my own.

Late in the afternoon I crash out in my room and listen to some music. My feet have backed off heaps from the morning. And that's the weird thing about it all, that's why I never go into it much with my mates or my olds or with anyone—'cause of the way it comes on and goes and seems to have a life of its own. One day I'm sore-footing around and having a big whinge to mysef, and the next it's back to just a bit of a niggle and I'm back out in the surf. If I made a drama of the bad days everyone would think I was just an A-grade put-on. So I don't. I've learned to just roll with it. When it gets too heavy duty I just back right off. "Hey Matt, where'd ya get to Sunday?—top surf." "Had a bit of a flu, Dills—had to shake it." But I know this, I'm sick of riding the rollercoaster. God, I'm looking forward to seeing the doc on Friday.

Next morning, I don't quite make the early. I wake with the light of the sunrise in my room. I can see a bit of beautiful-morning east-coast blue around the corner of the curtain, and I'm stoked already. I roll out of bed and test my feet on the floor—they're a little stiff, but they're all right. I go out the front to check out the day. The weather's lifted. The sou'easter's blown through. There's serious swell out there—I can feel its pulse in my veins, I can feel it shaking the shore. I swear there's a vibe that runs from the water up into me. I figure I'll go for a surf. It just clicks into place in my head and feels all right. I don't think I've said it aloud to myself yet, but I know I'm counting down. I know there's only so many surfs left, and then there'll be the op, and then there'll be a long—I don't know what—but I can bet I won't be catching many waves. I'll be laid up for a while. When I saw the doc, he said give it a year at least, that's the way it goes with major stuff like this. And after that, we'll see. And like I told you, he never said—I couldn't bear to ask—how hard I'd be able to smack a lip after it was all over. So that's all there, in the back of my head. Nothing I can change, and a whole lot of shit I'm going to have to learn to live with. And I'm still working on that.

The old lady's up and she says she doesn't need the car till one, so I take it. As I'm driving down the hill I can see the surf. It looks big. It looks huge. I know all the markers. I've been checking it out and measuring it for so long—against the highrise that runs down the hill, against the height of the Bower, against the Norfolks. I feel that mad joyous surge inside you get when you know it's really going off. That insane ecstatic rush. It's like you can't tear everything off and leap headfirst into the water fast enough. It's like this charge that starts to surge through you. I pull up down the beach where the crew hangs out and there's no one else around yet. It's still pretty early. A little before seven. Even as I step out of the car you can feel it. It's like the whole beach is shaking, there's a mist just hanging out there—over the surf, reaching over the shore—twenty foot high in the air like it only does when it's really big. There's that constant thunder that just fills all the air. I walk over to the wall and check it out.

It's too big. It's absolutely huge. It's all turned on. It's just a vast, mad, pounding arena of waves. There's no wind, so it's glassed off a bit, but it's too awesome to be workable. I go sit back on the bench, and just check it out for a bit. It's from the southeast. Big, high, fucking huge walls. Just non-stop pounding in. Steep, endlessly coming, gouging up the bottom sets. Way out, the Queensie bombie's going off—rolling big and high-peaked like it does in a good southerly. Breaking once, on the outside reef—fuller and thicker, then coursing deep and blue through the gully, and then re-forming and breaking again over the inside reef—with a heap more lip and barrel. A great fucking wicked curling barrel way out there in the middle of the bay that you could drive a garbo truck through—then it rolls into the deep again and heads for Queensie. And that's always a real heart-stopper—when you're out at Queensie Point and you see the bombie going off way outside, you know to get your head down and paddle till your heart aches, 'cause you're going to be looking at the greatest mother of a set in no time.

I watch it. There's no way you'd go out. The tide's too low. It's unrideable. It's just big walls slamming down. I see some head-case with a board under his arm walk down the beach way down at South Steyne, where it's a little smaller, and go in. I don't know where he's at—maybe he can see a shorey that looks okay or something. I watch him for a bit and the mad bastard looks like he's trying to get out the back—but he just keeps getting hammered and the rip's got so much suck it's taking him sideways up toward Mid Steyne twice as fast as he's paddling. He goes pretty much nowhere for fifteen minutes. I figure if the bastard ever gets out the back he'll be so knackered he'll be too wasted to take off on anything. I check my watch, tide's still going out for another hour—it's just going to keep getting uglier. I stand up on the bench and look above and past the beach break over to the Bower. I always love that first glimpse you get of it out there—big pockets coursing around the hub of the headland. This joy shoots up through me and I almost leap off the bench as I make out there's already a couple of guys out there. I don't need to think about it too long. I'm gone. I'm off that bench and into the car so fast it's not funny.

I get in the car and start to back out and flick the radio on at the same time, like you do. It's just one of those things you do—you're feeling a little juiced, a little buzzed, and you think you'll feed the rush you're on with a little noise. So I start down the road and they're just finishing the 7:30 news or something and the news guy's saying something like, *The names of the two young people killed in a horrific motor vehi-cle accident at Clontarf early on Sunday morning have not yet been released. The driver of the vehicle, an eighteen-year-old male, and the sole passenger, a fifteen-year-old female, were killed when their vehicle—a late model Porsche—ran off the road and struck a rock wall. Police are continuing their inves-tigations . . .*

I hear it; and this sick flood, this mad quake of knowing runs through me, shakes me. I shake so badly, I nearly run off the road. I manage to hook the car over into the curb, and just sort of seize up there. I'm trying to breathe, I'm still trying to hear. But the news is over. There's nothing more. I feel like I'm going to throw up. There's some music—I stab the radio off. I sit there—totally freaking out. My mind blinded. A shaking cold sweat creeping all over me. I've never freaked out so much in my life. I swear, I'll never forget those seconds—when I flicked the radio on. And I feel trapped there—the car running—nose stabbed into the curb, but I can't move. I feel like something's been rammed up against my chest, crushing it, pinning me there. I feel like I'm going a little mad, not being able to think straight, not knowing for sure. I hang my head. I crush my eyes shut.

"Son."

I look up. It's a fucking cop. It's like you wouldn't credit it. I crack up and run off the road, and a cop shows up. I swear, I almost let out a mad cackle.

"What's happening, son? You all right? You're halfway out in the middle of the road here."

"I'm okay."

He leans in and looks a little closer at me.

"Want to step out here out of the car for a minute."

"I just heard the news."

He watches me. He doesn't say anything. But he's got this look.

"—Down at Clontarf—the accident."

He pauses, and studies me, "What accident?" But I can tell by his face he knows what I'm on about.

"Do you know their names? Is it Hayley Churchill and Lewis Castor? Do you know that . . .?"

"I can't tell you that. It's not released yet. They're still trying to contact the boy's parents . . ."

This guy's a young cop, I reckon he's only about twenty-one or -two, and he's given all the stiff cop shit away in one when I say Hayley's name. He just can't hide it.

"Were you down there?" I say.

"Listen mate, I can't talk to you about it now—"

"Listen, I took her to the party—Saturday night—Hayley Churchill . . . me. I took her to the party . . . and I was supposed to take her home, except she went off with some other guy . . ."

"Mate, I'm sorry."

"Well it's fucking obvious, isn't it. It's pretty fucking obvious."

"Listen, son, calm down. I know you're upset, but calm down, all right."

"Listen—just say 'no' if it isn't. Just say fucking anything. Honestly, who fucking cares . . . Jesus Christ—Hayley's dead— *oh shit*—I can't believe it . . . I haven't seen her since then . . ."

You should see the expression on his face. It's like someone's died in his arms. He looks like he doesn't know what to do with me.

"This is unreal. Oh Christ, this is mad—I've got to call Drewe . . ."

"Listen mate, I want you to step out of the car for a minute here, okay. All right. That's what I'm asking you to do. Just leave it there and step out of the car."

I drag my arse out of there. I couldn't give a fuck anymore. I'm totally wasted. I'm reeling. I figure if he realizes I'm not loaded or on something he's going to leave me alone. But I don't know what I'm going to do after that. I'm actually fearful of that. I'm fearful of the moments that are going to come after. What do I do? Where do I go? I can feel it rising in me. As I get out of the car the fear is really starting to overwhelm me—what am I going to do? I stand by the front of the car, leaning back against it. He asks for my license, and I give it to him. He's checking me out.

"You all right?"

"Yeah. *No.* I don't know. It's Hayley Churchill, isn't it? Oh God . . . Just tell me, will you—please . . . she's dead—oh God . . ."

"Had a few drinks or a smoke or something with your mates?"

"Listen mate, I'm not all right. I'm fucking cracking up here. The babe I took to a party on Saturday night I just heard on the radio is dead. I'm fucking freaking out here . . ."

"What's the story, constable?"

The other cop's out of the car and coming over. He's a big burly red-faced looking bastard.

"He knows the girl in the car down at Clontarf. Just heard it on the radio."

"I don't *know* her—I fuckin' grew up with her! Her fuckin' brother's my best fuckin' mate! I fuckin' took her to that bloody party on Saturday night!" It occurs to me at some point I'm yelling. Yelling my head off. But I don't care. I'm past caring. If they want to arrest me or give me a ticket or what the fuck, I don't fucking care. I've got these awful waves of terror, of desperation, that keep hitting me. I feel a well of feeling so awful beginning to overwhelm me. It feels like the most nauseating, sickening fear.

"Listen mate, calm down. Get a hold of yourself or we're going to have to run you down the station."

The young cop goes, "This is Senior Constable Mike Rafters, and I'm Constable Jeff Peters—of the Northern Highway Patrol. What's your name?" He looks down at my license, he's still got it in his hand.

"Matt. Matt Owen."

"Matt, you were at that party down at Queenscliff on Saturday night, were you—that these two young people were at? Is that right?—is that what you're telling us?"

"Yeah."

"What happened?"

"I took Hayley—oh God, this isn't real. I can't believe this . . ."

"Matt, I'm going to park your car in here properly. Then I want you to come down to the station with us and answer a few questions about Hayley's death, okay. There's some more information the police still need to know. We may want you to give us a statement about what you saw . . ."

I look at him. I have the strangest feeling. I feel suddenly like I'm absent. Like I'm removed. I feel like I'm sort of observing what's going on from somewhere else. It occurs to me as I look at this young cop's face that I got up to go for a surf and now a cop's asking me for a statement.

"There's no point."

"Why not, Matt?"

"I didn't see anything—I hardly saw her all night. I picked her up—we had a blue in the car—I dropped her off down at the party. I only spoke to her once again all night—and Drewe was there. Fuck, this is not real . . ."

"Matt. We'd still like you to come down the station so we can talk to you properly."

"No! Fuck it! There's no fucking point!" I'm so angry. I've never been so angry in all my life. You wouldn't credit it, the only time in my life I'm blowing a fuse and it's got to be with a couple of cops. It's like something's gone wrong in me, something's clicked over, and I can't control it. I never get angry. I'm known as the most laid-back bastard on the planet. I start walking away, up onto the grass. I'm so angry, I'm afraid of what I'm going to do or say with the cops. I just want to get away. I just want to cry or scream.

I look away and I get a bright, blinding glimpse of the massive surf. And I hear the cop say behind me, "Matt. Two young people died—two of your friends. The police need help with their investigation. There's some suggestion of drugs. We need to know how much they drank and whatever else was going on. We need to know that for their families—to give them some peace of mind."

I'm still angry, and I don't even know why. But I've cooled down a little. I'm hanging onto it. I turn around to the cop. "There were no drugs. Hayley drank vodka and orange, and shit like that all night, I think . . . Lew never did anything—he hardly drank . . . But not now," I say. "I'm too freaked out. I'll come down later, I promise. I'm too freaked out right now."

They're both standing there, up on the grass, watching me. "All right," the senior one says. "Constable Peters will give you his card. We're asking you to contact him in the next couple of days, and come down and have a talk with us. Okay?"

"Okay."

"You got the name?" the senior cop says to the other.

He gives a nod, as he's writing in his book. "Matt," the junior cop says as he hands me my license back, "we need to talk to you. If I don't hear from you, we'll give you a call—"

"Okay," I say. I feel as hollow as a cardboard box. I feel

turned over and emptied out. I couldn't care if they raid my house and arrest my sister. I'm walking away. I just want to get away. From everything.

I start over to the wall. And they turn and walk back to their car. There seems something missing in their manner. It's like they don't know quite how to handle me.

I stand there for a minute by the wall looking out over the surf. It looks to me just then the most desolate place I have ever seen. The fear is back. Rising like water over my head. I don't know where to go. I don't know what to do. I get this pang of feeling absolutely desperate and alone.

I get back in the car. Back up, and start driving down toward Mid Steyne. I don't know where I'm driving. I'm just going. I couldn't stand there any longer by the wall, by the surf. I couldn't hold onto the grief.

I drive through Manly and around to the Bower. It's no logical or apparent decision I make. I just do it. It just seems to happen. I park in the parking lot at the top of the headland where I always do and get out and stand at the railing that is high at the bluff edge of the cliff face, and gaze out over the ocean and down at the thundering madness on the rocks below. "Hayley's dead," I say, with soft disbelief, out into the still air. "Hayley's dead," I say again. I look out at the sea. It does not reply. The sun is blasting its brightness through the mist of the big swell and the last thin cloud of the bad weather. The hotness and wetness are beginning to rise, and the ocean is a sprawling, charging web of great waves below. It feels like the world has ended. And all of this can try to defy that all it likes—but it fails. The world has still ended.

A car lurches into the car park behind me. Five boards on top, five guys inside. They burst out of the car, and hurtle madly toward the path that leads through the bush and out to the crest of the headland where you check out the break. I'm still thinking, still talking to the great empty drop of air out from the cliff edge. "Hayley's dead," I tell it again, softly, insanely. God, what's happened to Drewe? I think suddenly. And at the same time, a thing in my head, a part of me keeps going, "It can't be. It just can't be." It's like a counter-mantra. Every time I say "Hayley's dead" I hear this dull chant from somewhere in me, "No, it can't be. It can't be." But I know she is. I can feel it. Standing there at the Bower looking at the rising brilliant light, and the mad swirling sea, I know she is now. Hayley's dead. How can it be? It felt like we were all immortal.

I carry my board along the damp brown path, that twists and winds between the rocks and bush, down and around the headland to the water. Silent, past the guys from the car, standing at the lookout now, watching the ocean in quiet disbelief. I feel the soft brown earth between my toes as I go. Feel life. Sharply. Strangely. I don't know what I'm doing. I'm actually thinking to myself, *I've gone nuts.* I don't know why I'm doing it. Hayley's dead, and I'm going out in the water. But it's the only place I can see to go. I don't want to go and phone. I don't want to go and see. I don't want to be there at the start of it all—the talk, the tears, the hell of who did what, of what went wrong. I just want to go out into the sea. And be there.

When I first hit the water I think of Lew properly, clearly, for the first time. Lew enters my head like he hasn't before now. Lew was going to be a property developer. Lew was going to be driving a Ferrari and retired at thirty-one. If you voted most likely to succeed at the end of Year Twelve, Lew would have scooped the poll. Lew's dead too. The whole thing sort of spins and comes at me from a new way. Hayley's dead. Lew's dead. They had barely started.

The surf's so big it snaps me out of it. It's coming so hard and huge around the rocks by the old jetty I have to paddle south first, back around toward Shelley Beach, to get around it. I've seen the Bower big before, but never been out in it quite like this. I saw it in a winter storm swell once—so big the sets were breaking up the walkway that runs around the foreshore from Manly. The next day great slabs of asphalt and concrete were flipped and strewn like cards along the shore. It took the council about half a year to repair it all. I go left and left and just keeping going out and around as far as I have to to get around it. I just keep paddling in the midst of this mad churning wash that's just tossing me all over the place. Through the foam that's strewn white and gray and all shitty 'cause it's so big and it can't stop tearing everything up. But I don't really feel a fear. I feel a strange friendship. A knowing. I know this place. I know it out here. I know the color and shape of the rock bottom all around the headland. I know how the water passes over it—I know the shapes it makes. I feel a sort of ease. It's where I want to be.

There's two guys out. I can see them way way out the back, halfway over into the channel. I watch them against the size of a set that comes through. A huge silver-gray wave, like a mountain shifting. They bob and rise, and then drop out of view. For a moment it's like this calm reason comes into my head. What are you doing out here? It's too big. It's too big to ride. But it goes. It's like there's something I want to do, something I have to do. I just want to be out in it for a while. I keep working to the left—further and further out into the channel with each set, going over and over to get around it—giving it all the room I can. The two small black shapes way out the back of the break appear and disappear—rising up the sets as they rear up over the rock shelf, forming in that thick double-peaked way the wave at the Bower does. As I paddle the whole scene sends a surge, a mad shake through me. It's so immense, so awesome—it drives this exhilaration into you. One of the dark shapes out the back drops into the shoulder of a wall—cruises a distance on the safe corner of the wall—then glides up and over the back and is gone before the blue-gray mountain hits the real shelf and really starts to thunder. An instant later, I watch the same wave barrel by me—a great mind-blowing cylindrical grinding. I feel like my heart has been torn out of me. I feel free.

I'm most of the way out the back, so I start to work over just a little from the channel back in toward the break. Just a bit, I say to myself. I figure I've gone a little too far out, and I need to come back a bit—or I'll end up halfway out to sea. And just as I'm doing that, it occurs to me I haven't really sussed out the big sets properly and where they're really coming as well as I should have, and maybe I'm going over a little soon. And right then, I see this absolutely massive wave coming, and I realize I've totally blown it. I've misjudged it totally—I've come too far back inside too soon. I feel the water drawing around me, feel the surge of the wave coming, just sucking all the water away, just drawing me further into the impact zone, and I start dying in the arse. All present and past and what happened this morning and every other thing becomes an absolute nothing. I'm looking at the biggest wave I've ever seen. I'm looking at the absolute hammering of a lifetime. I can't believe I've been so dumb. There's this fucking wave coming that's so big and so solid blue and so high and wide it's the biggest thing I've ever seen anywhere, and I just start going, *Ah, you're ratshit.* And I keep paddling 'cause there's nothing else to do, I'm in the absolute impact zone—I can't back up—I'm too close. I can only try to scrape through it. And I'm dying in the arse. This wave is going to hammer me like nothing before.

I roll, just as it starts to peel. And if you've rolled under enough waves you have a sense of where you are, you know how it is. There's that little bit too far inside where it feels sort of flat and dead and you're going to cop the most absolute bone-crushing impact; and there's that little bit further outside where you're deeper into the wave and you can just scrape through with the worst of it rolling over you and it just sucks you back. Well, I roll in the flat spot, that dead sucky spot where the whole house is about to fall on your head. And while you're hanging there, there's always this pause, this split second that goes on forever, when it's like nothing's happening, while some great lip is curling overhead, coming driving down toward you, and you're down there, waiting. You drift, in that awful stillness, and then it's like someone puts a bomb under you—and it all goes off. It just hammers you down—and you go up and over, and you go down and round, you get hurled and smashed and rolled, over and over and over. But what happens with this one is with my board—it just flies away from my arms. Rips free of my hands. As the first big impact hits me, I feel it break into two. It just separates, and flings away—like a bird, tearing away from me. Ripping free and flying. And then it's gone. Flung. Snatched. And I'm on my own, going over and over, waiting for it to let me up, going over and over, the lack of air starting to throb and well green and purple in my head and chest. And all the time I'm trying to keep my head off the rock bottom.

I come up in the white, ripped, boiling wash—halfway back around the Racecourse. Black rocks too near to my left. Lungs ripped, chest exploding, head full of black splotches. Body heaving as big spinning lines of wash keep rolling over me. But it's all right, I can handle this I tell myself. I know how to do this. I just let it roll over me and I go down between each set and come up when it lets me, and let it push me the rest of the way around the point. You don't fight it. You just hang on and let it take you till it quits.

I drift around past the jetty, I don't even swim, I'm too hammered to swim. I just float and squirt water and let the last lines of wash push and roll over me. I don't bother trying to get in at the jetty—it's too big—you'd just get banged up on the rocks. I go all the way around to Shelley Beach.

I drift up onto the shore there, and sit—in the calmness of the shallows—the water at my waist. I look back across to the break. From Shelley Beach you can only see the end of the section, but that's enough. I watch it all white torn and thundering and relentless. I catch sight of the tail end of my board—banging over against the rock face of the walkway that runs back around to Manly. I glance down at the snapped tail end of my leg rope, trailing underwater at my ankle. I sit there in the water. Watching it all. Feeling the sun on my face, feeling my feet in the gluggy sand under the water.

"You know, you didn't have to do that," I say to myself.

And I feel the warm, gentle lull of water around me.

I look back again. Across the blue sheen of water to the distance of the break.

"Last wave," I say.

CHAPTER EIGHT

"THE DOCTOR CALLED," DELIA SAYS, AS I COME IN the door, with just the tail end of my board in my hand. "He wants to move your operation forward to this Friday." She looks at the board. "What happened?"

"Ah—busted it."

I stand there, all worked over and smashed about and drained out, and look at her. I think how people can't know where each other have been or what's happened to them—how maybe it's a wonder people can get across to each other at all sometimes. It must be awful to come home from a war.

"Mum—you hear the news this morning?"

"No, what news? I was out walking."

"Hayley—and a mate of mine—they were killed in a car accident down at Clontarf—on Saturday night."

Delia's putting the orange juice back in the fridge or something like that. And she turns and looks at me—with this drained, devastated look on her face. Then she just drops the juice. Lets it go. It's the strangest thing—it's like she just totally loses it for an instant. The container slides from her hand and hits the floor at her feet and splits on impact and spreads an explosion of orange across the floor. "Oh my God," she says, looking over at me.

Around ten I try to phone Drewe, but the phone's busy. I try again around 10:30, and eleven, and 11:30, and so on. It just rings busy all the time, I think they've taken it off the hook. I phone the doctor. I speak to his secretary. She says he wants to operate this Friday and I say I think that's okay but she wants to put me through to him. "Matt, one of my patients dropped out of the list this Friday—I'd like to move you up. That okay with you?"

I swear I love this guy. I love the simple lingo he speaks. He doesn't stuff around—he just tells me what's going on. He calls me Matt. Half the bastards I went to before him had their heads so far up their arses they wouldn't even say hello to me.

A part of me almost hesitates. I want to say, "A friend of mine's just died. I'm not sure." But I don't. I don't seem able to. I just don't seem able to say the words. Somewhere, in my heart, I know it doesn't matter anymore. It's too late. And I don't want to fuck around—not him or me. I want so desperately to get on with this. "Yeah, that's fine. What do I have to do?" He gives me the drill. Delia's sitting there on the sofa when I put the phone down. "Looks like I'm going in for my op on Friday," I say to her.

Delia looks all pale. I've never seen her look so bad. "Matt, what happened with Hayley?"

I look at her. "She went off with some guy—a mate of mine she was keen on—and I think they crashed into a rock wall down at Clontarf."

She sits there looking at me. She just looks totally bewildered. "I thought you were together?" she says at last.

"We were—for about eight minutes. Then we split up."

Delia's still looking at me wide eyed and sort of strange. Her eyes sort of bulging.

"It just happened, Mum. There was nothing I could do."

"Are you all right?"

"Yeah, I think so. I don't know. I'm really freaking out. But I don't know what I can do about it." I gaze down at the phone. "I ran into some cops down the beach this morning—they want to talk to me."

She makes a little movement, all ruffled and uncertain. "Is that okay? You can speak to your father, you know . . . your father has friends . . ."

"It's fine Mum, nothing was going on. We just went our own ways . . . I don't even know anything. This guy gets around in his old man's Porsche all the time—I don't even know what went on."

I don't know what Delia's thinking. She was going to go off

to tennis or something but she isn't now. She looks like there's something she wants to do but she doesn't know how to do it.

"Mum, there's nothing you can do."

We sit in silence for moment. She starts to cry, and her eyes have gone all red, and she wipes her eyes and her nose with a tissue. I want to comfort her, but I can't. I can't lift myself. I feel like my heart's been struck. And I know I'm the one that's in real strife here. The one that's really for it.

"I've got to talk to Drewe."

"Yes, of course you do."

I dial the Churchills' number again, it's busy. I knew it would be. I've got to go down there, I think to myself. Just the suggestion makes me feel sick. It makes my whole world reel. How can I just walk in there? But I've got to see them. I've got to talk to them and tell them what happened. I try to think of myself walking up to them. I can't, the thought just makes my world lurch.

"Can I use the car?"

"Of course."

"I've got to go see Drewe—and Hayley's folks."

"Of course, honey, just take it, go. But be careful."

I walk out the front of my place and get to the gate and Drewe pulls into the curb. It's like some kind of weird synchronized thing. I go over to the passenger's side window and look in at him. He gives me this funny sort of half look, sort of half at me and half away, sort of like it would be too painful to look at anyone directly or say anything.

I get in. He crunches the gears a bit and pulls away slowly. We go through the Fairlight shops and start down the hill and neither of us have spoken. We're just there in silence. There's the sound of the engine inside the car, there's the sound of the day and the traffic outside. He goes through the back streets to the beach and then straight across the road at Mid Steyne and pulls into the beach at the first place he can. We sit there, in silence, the surf, the distant silver blue of the ocean out in front of us. Then he speaks:

"I had to let you know, mate. I thought it was unfair on you."

"Thanks, mate . . ."

"The cops reckon he was doing 190 clicks. Reckon he just lost it in the dip. They took us down and showed us the wall."

"Oh shit—"

"They're talking about some shit too."

"Like what?"

"Like coke."

"*What*—?" I almost shout.

"Yeah. Some shit about it—I don't know where they got it from. It's got to be bullshit . . ."

"Are you fucking kidding—"

"They did some blood tests after the crash. Apparently they've got to if someone gets hurt. And they reckon something turned up. So now they're doing the full bit and waiting for the report—my fuckin' olds are freaking out . . ."

"Oh fuck."

We sit in silence.

"I keep thinking about your folks. God, I just want to cry."

"Ah mate—" He puts a hand up to his face, over his eyes. "Ah mate," he says again. "Sunday morning the old man's in a frenzy—Hayls isn't home and he's ready to take off up the hill and kick your arse—then the cops knock on the door. Mate, I was standing there—it was the sickest moment of my life."

"Oh fuck."

"She went through the windscreen, mate—I went with the old man to ID her—oh Hayley . . ." he says in a sighed whisper that's so sad.

I can't bear to make a sound. I can't squeak, or I'll just burst into tears.

Drewe sits in silence again, like he's watching the far blue, but he isn't. Then he says, "You know, right down by the reserve at Clonnie—where the road sort of comes down one side and down the other—a big sort of dip—and there's a big rock wall all along on your right—right there, mate—just totally lost it . . . fuckin' weird spot—what were they doin' down there." He chokes a little. He puts his hand up over his face again like he's going to cry. "Mate, we did the full tour . . ."

I just sit there. I can't bear to speak.

"I know this is hard, mate—but don't come down to the house for a bit, okay. Everyone's too freaked out. The doc's put Mum on something, he had to, she cracked up. Just leave it a bit, hey. They know it's not your fault—I told them what went on—but just leave it for a bit."

"I have to say something to them."

"I know you have to. But just give it a couple of days."

I think about it. What will I possibly say to them? Your daughter gave me the flick, so I wasn't there when she died? What can I possibly say that will be of any value now that their daughter's dead? There's nothing. Hayley got to the party because of me. Hayley and me set it up. One way or another.

Drewe's watching me.

"Matt, Owl. Listen, mate. It's not your fault. No one's ever going to say it is. Everyone knows what happened—knows what Hayley was like. Do you hear me? Even my old man doesn't blame you—I told them what happened—I told them the way she pissed you off the moment you got back to the car—"

"*Great story, hey.* Fuckin' brilliant story . . . Drewe, I should have been looking out for her."

"Matt, we were looking out for her. Stop having yourself on. You couldn't have done any more than you did, any more than I could have told her what to do—we *were* looking out for Hayley—as far as anyone fucking could—and you and I both know that's the truth. But it still fucking happened."

But it doesn't seem to help. It makes no difference at all. I did it. Me and Hayls. At that point, I feel like I can't imagine life ahead of me anymore. It feels stopped and meaningless. It doesn't spread out into the future like it used to. It ends right there. It appears over, now. I can't imagine that it will possibly go on and anything that ever matters will ever happen again. I feel like I've died.

"Mate, it just happened. It was just a freaking fucking thing."

Yeah, I guess so, I think to myself. *A freaking fucking thing.* I hope at best to be able to think of it that way for the rest of my life.

We sit there. The babes go by on their roller blades. The young groms go by carrying their boards.

"Thanks for coming up."

"That's all right. I had to—"

He's checking me out. I don't say anything. There's nothing there.

"I'll give you a call, okay . . . about the funeral . . . you know . . . shit like that . . ."

I sit there a while, looking out at the sea, through the windscreen. "I wish I could say something to your olds."

"There's nothing you can, mate. It just happened. Just leave it a bit, okay."

Drewe says he has to go, and says he'll drop me back up the hill. But I say no, and get out of the car. I stand there on the walkway at Mid Steyne with the nor'easter flickering around me and making that noise it does up high in the Norfolks. There feels a movement to everything, I think I can feel the earth ever so slowly turning. That slow grinding spinning of a great world. I don't know where to go. I don't know why I didn't let Drewe drop me back home. I can't identify the parts of me that feel lost, but they're not the obvious parts, they're not the things you can easily put your finger on and say this is gone and I feel like this, this has happened and it has left me this way. It feels so different from that. When someone died I never thought it would feel like this. I never thought I'd stand on the bright grass by the surf and stare at a green picnic table. I walk over to the picnic table and sit up on it. I'm not sure how long I sit there with my head in my hands, not thinking anything. I feel like I've been stripped bare. There seems nothing worth offering, nothing to say or do. I'd walk down to North Steyne, but I don't know who might be there, and I don't want to talk, I don't want to stir the ashes. Not just yet, maybe never.

I sit there alone under the great Norfolks for as long as I can bear it, then I get up and walk back through Manly to the bus stop. I don't feel like walking up the hill. I pass a newsagent on the way. There's those yellowish posters out the front in wire frames: "Teenage Car Crash—Drugs Involved." I have this great urge to go over and take the poster, I have no idea why. I would keep it, I would fold it into a book, and in twenty years I might look at it and understand, but I don't. I just keep walking. And I sit at the bus stop and wait for the bus.

The phone rings. As I'm walking through to the kitchen. I'm not really walking through to the kitchen. I'm just sort of wandering around—trying to hold off cracking up. I pick it up. I don't know why. I don't really want to. But I'm right by it, so I do. If I hadn't been right by it, I would have just let it ring.

"Hi, Matt—"

"Hi—"

"—It's Emy."

"Oh hi—"

"How are you?"

"Yeah, I'm okay. I'm all right." My voice is sort of croaky and I try to smooth it out but I can't seem to.

She hesitates. Like I've sort of put her off or something.

"Sorry, Em. I'm still a little weird."

"It's all right. You okay?"

"I guess. Still really freaked out."

"You getting some help?"

"I tell you, Em, they get me any more help, I'm going to need treatment for the help." I give a croaky little laugh. And she laughs too. I think that makes us both feel a little better.

"They're all having a drink," she pauses, "tonight."

"God, it's nice to hear your voice," I say, "it's like a fresh breeze." I'm thinking, it's like getting down the beach and feeling the salt air on your face after you've been locked inside for a month.

She's quiet. Like maybe I've embarrassed her.

"Sorry, I didn't mean to embarrass you. Just ignore me. It's just what I felt."

"It's not that, you just made me cry."

"Oh. Sorry."

I wait. I can hear her wiping her nose or something.

"So what do you think about this drink?" she says, in a strained unintentionally clowny kind of voice. "Pete Ryan's arranged it. He says it's kind of a wake for Hayley and Lewis . . ."

For Hayley and Lewis, that bit jags like a great barb in my side. But I unhook myself from it, and keep moving.

"Yeah . . . guess it sounds okay. Where? Down the Steyne?"

"Uh-huh. Most of them are already down there. Do you want a ride? Natalie's driving. We can pick you up."

"No, it's all right. I'll get down there. I'll see you down there, okay?"

"Okay. We'll be there around eight."

"Okay."

She pauses. "You going to come?"

My turn to pause. "Yeah, I will."

"I wish I could see you . . . just to talk or something."

"Believe me, Em—nothing can help this."

She's quiet.

"I'll come, Em. I promise. I'd really like to see you too. You're about one of the two people on the planet I actually want to see."

I put the phone down thinking, so dumbly, so simply, how she just sounds so nice on the phone. So sweet and nice. Her voice feels like it soothes something. It's such a weird thought. But it's too true to deny. The whole thing feels so skewed right at that instant. I'm sort of thinking what an angel she sounds like on the phone and how it makes me feel a little better and how I've never had a girl call me up and just talk to me like that on the phone. I wish it was another time, I say to myself.

And I don't feel so sure about a *kind of wake.* It just feels dumb to me. And in between all the cracking up with all this,

I feel like I've reached some sort of limit when it comes to dumb. With the unraveling and the raving that's gone on in the last couple of days since Hayley's death I feel like I've had enough dumb to last me a lifetime. I don't want a drink. I don't want to get blind. Not in the name of Hayls and Lew, or anything else. It would just be another dumb thing, compounded on all the others. But then I think about Emy, and all the guys in the crew, and how there's nothing dumb or bullshit about any of that, and that makes me know I should just go with it. It almost makes some kind of sense. I'll drink a few cold, sharp beers and get a little banged in the head and think about Hayls and Lew—so out of their skulls and cranked-up mad-arse tearing about they smacked into a wall and totaled themselves. That'll do, I tell myself. That passes for some kind of logic. I think I'm still cracking up just a little.

I don't make the pub till after nine. I start down the hill, and I lose the plot. About halfway down Hayls comes into my head—so vivid and sharp and beautiful, that this rush of emotion, of sadness, just decks me. I just want to go home, and lie on my bed in the dark and cry. And there doesn't seem a stupider thing I could do, than to be going down to the pub to have a drink in some way to do with her death. So I turn around and head home. But then I get back up to the shops at Fairlight—and you know that way your feelings can swing so suddenly, the way they can grab you and send you reeling over to the flipside of what you felt, well, it happens just like that— all of a sudden I'm just thinking I'm being so stupid and piss-weak, and I'm bailing out on my mates. And it seems to me if I don't go for a drink with my mates, I'm just about the most mixed-up, piss-weak bastard that ever lived. So I turn around, and head back down the hill. And on the way I'm thinking about the brown curves of Hayley's elbows and shoulders, and the dirty honey sheen of her skin by the end of summer. And that look in her eyes. That darkness and light and sharpness—that was always there—appraising you, pushing you, giving you heaps, fooling you. I can't work out how that light can be gone. She was just so full of life. She would have grown older and just become more of that way she was. I just can't get that. I'll never get it.

I go in through the public deliberately and buy a schooner at the bar. I don't normally go near the public—I hate it, it's always full of slaggy old bastards who reek like old dogs, but I go in the public and stand at the bar and drink a little of a beer. I stay at the bar and drink some more. I get stuck there. I can't lift myself to move. I've gotten lost again, my feelings have turned back on me again. I stand at the bar fixed like a fence post and I drink most of the beer. I start thinking, I'll finish it and walk out of there, and go home. I'm feeling real bad again. I don't think I can face the crowd. The talk. The questions. The chatter. In the end, Hayley's dead, and I was supposed to be taking her and bringing her home, and nothing will ever change any of that. It doesn't matter what Drewe says, all that will never change. I stood there and told her folks I'd bring her home. And I didn't. I didn't bring Hayley home. And she'll never come home. And all I want to do is howl. I want to stand right there at the bar and let out the saddest, longest howl you've ever heard. Like one of those dogs you hear in your neighborhood that's been tied up all day and it's breaking its heart, its spirit, its everything. I want to let out the saddest, longest howl of grief. But I can't. I don't. Then I see Dills on the other side of the bar—it's one of those circular bars in the middle of the floor. He spots me and comes over.

"Matt, how are ya, mate? You hangin' in there?"

"Yeah. I'm okay."

He checks me out for an instant. "Drewe came down, mate."

"—Yeah?"

"Yeah. He's out there with all the guys."

"Didn't think he would."

"Yeah, me neither . . ."

We stand there, and I look at my beer, 'cause I can't really handle looking at anything else. Then I just speak up. It's like it comes out of me involuntarily. "I don't think I can hack what I did, Dills . . ."

"Don't be like that, mate . . . no one's blaming you . . . no one . . ."

"Yeah, well, maybe they don't need to—"

"—I mean it, mate—it was just bad news."

"I'd be fuckin' retarded not to . . ."

"No you wouldn't, mate . . . You were unlucky—you were just too close to it. It's like standing on a corner and some kid suddenly bolts out and gets run over—unless you're fuckin' Superman—there's nothing you can do . . ."

"I wish I was fuckin' Superman."

Dills gives a sort of sad laugh. "Don't we all . . ."

I almost crack a smile.

We stand there. Dills doesn't go. But I still sort of wish he would. It's a little better but it's still pretty bad.

"You reckon Lew was to the eyeballs on coke . . . ?" I say.

"Lew never did shit like that, Owl. You know that. He drove like a mad bastard but he never did shit like that."

"Yeah, it's true isn't it. You know, Dills, the whole thing doesn't make any fuckin' sense."

"No, it doesn't, does it. It's the stupidest maddest thing I've ever seen."

We just stand there. Both bewildered.

"If Lew was ripped—I'll be fucked," says Dill. "I knew the bastard—it's bullshit."

"You did know him—didn't you. You two played water polo in the same team for like six years . . ."

"Mate, we were together in the nippers down at Freshie from the age of six. He didn't do any shit. They're going to change their story . . . or it's just bullshit . . ."

"You reckon?"

"I don't *reckon*. I *know*. It's coming."

Dills sips his beer thoughtfully.

"I was never that close with Lew," I say. "There was always a sort of distance between us."

"He could be a bit of a wanker sometimes—we both knew that. He thought you were cool, Owl. He always reckoned you surfed pretty hot . . ."

"Yeah? We just never seemed to get on like some of the other guys in the crew."

"Mate, he had his head up his arse half the time—thinking what a *ledge* he was—but he was still a good guy. Can you believe the bastard's dead? Fuck—we were little nippers, mate, divin' for flags—just Lew and me—and I'd never even heard of half you bastards. And now the bastard's gone. My old man's so cut up, mate—he used to take us—every Sunday—" Dills pauses "—it just sucks."

Dills stands there a moment, one hand rested on the bar, thinking about it all. You can see the hurt, the pain, running through his face. Then he turns to me. "Drewe was saying he's about to go—reckon you want to say g'day before he splits?"

"Yeah."

Dills buys a few more drinks. He wants me to get into the round, but I don't want to. I don't feel like drinking, but I buy another beer just for something to hang on to. I'm thinking about seeing the rest of the crew. I don't know how to do this, I don't want to know how to do it. I follow him out into the beer garden. I feel so much trepidation, so much anxiety—and that's so dumb 'cause I've known half these guys since primary school. I don't know why.

It's like everybody's there. It's like a Saturday night session, but it's not—the rest of the pub's sort of half deserted. There's two tables pulled together and everyone's around them, just like we always do—all the crew, lots of the babes. But it's not buzzing like usual. It's sort of desolate and half-pissed and sad. A few of the guys look just totally wasted. They look like they've hit it so hard already they're just totally gone. Stink looks up as I come up to the table and he gives me a sort of shit-faced jerky acknowledgment. Spears is smoking a bent cigarette and telling a story about how one time the ranger tried to bust us for lighting a fire on the beach and Lew started coming back at him and telling him what the council regs were and by the end of it the guy couldn't get out of there fast enough. It was true, Lew was like that, he was real ballsy, he had respect for nothing, he'd get in anyone's face. That's what I couldn't hack about him sometimes, he was always so sure of himself. But Spears' story is a good one. It recalls Lew truly.

Emy's there, and I go and sit by her. I want to be by her. "Hi, Matt," she says lightly as I sit down, and I say hi to her and Natalie. Drewe's right across from me and I can see him sort of checking me out. "You okay, mate?" he says.

"Yeah, I'm okay," I tell him. And I stick my face in my beer glass, to cover up whatever it is I'm doing that's making everyone else worry.

"Didn't know if you'd be down," I say to Drewe.

"Had to, mate—needed to get out for a bit of air—it's not so hot at home—"

"—Yeah . . ."

And then I realize that Layla's beside him. She smiles at me, "Hey Matt," she says.

"Hey, Layla, how's it goin'?"

"I'm cool, Matt. How about you?"

"Yeah—like you'd expect, you know—I'm fucked . . . I'm fucking coming undone I think . . ."

"You all right, mate?" Drewe says.

"Yeah, I'm all right. I just killed your fucking sister."

"Matt, come on—cut it out—all right. Come on—you're all right."

"Sure I'm fucking all right. Hayley's dead. But I'm all right."

Drewe goes stumm. He just sits there, looking at me. Flat at me. Not mad or angry or anything. But just flat and level at me. Gets the message over that way. It's like—*stop fucking with me, bro, things are bad enough as it is.* It's like—*if you're my bro, cut it out now.* And I get it. And I knock it all off. It reminds me that this is the present. This is the here and now. And you can start fucking with that too. But it just makes you a bigger wanker.

"I'm sorry," I say to him. "I'm all right. It just got to me a bit. I'm sorry."

"You're cool, mate. You're cool, Matt. Don't be sorry."

And I feel the water pool in the back of my eyes. But I hold it back.

Dills says something, kind of dives in and saves it and takes it away somewhere else, and it all kind of goes away for a bit and I find myself looking at Layla. Checking her out. My God, she's got the most amazing set of boobs. But apart from that I can't really work out anything that looks pregnant about her. I'm wondering what's happening with this biz with Drewe and her. But I can't tell a thing.

"Mate, we got to get going . . ." Drewe says, getting up. "I gotta drop Layla home." He looks at me. "Stay cool, hey mate."

"Yeah. I'm all right. Sorry about the shit."

"There was no shit, mate. Just take it easy on yourself. You know what I'm saying?"

"Yeah, I know. I will."

"Do it for me, okay Matt."

"Okay."

"See you, Matt," Layla says, as she gets up.

"See you, Layla. Good to see you."

Drewe just kind of hangs there for a sec before he goes, and looks at me. "It's looking like Friday week, mate . . ." he says, kind of pacing the way he says it, taking it steady, " . . . for Hayley." He pauses. "It's a little slow 'cause of the police stuff . . ."

I just sort of nod. I can't find any noise to make.

He reaches down and takes up his glass, and empties it, "Take it easy, hey guys . . ." he says to everyone, and then he goes with Layla.

There's an inebriated chorus of farewells. And I really realize how badly smashed just about all the rest of the crew are. It looks like they sort of went at it hell for leather earlier—and now they're in the crash-out zone. Croc's down the far end and he's put his head sideways down on the table like he's after a particular view of something like a bug that's crawling up a nearby wall. Stink's lighting a cigarette at the wrong end and he's got Shaz hanging off the side of him trying to get it from him, and I think he's looking at me, but he's got that sort of befuddled, smudgy look he gets in his eyes when he's really wasted, and I don't think he's seeing me at all.

"They're still an item, hey?" Dills says to me—cocking his head in the direction Drewe and Layla just left in.

"Think so."

"Wouldn't credit it, hey?"

"You said it."

Dills looks about. "Looks like we're the only ones standing, hey mate."

"What time the rest of them rock up?"

"Round four they reckon—earlier. Spears reckoned Stink started flat out on the double scotches—and he was on his ear by five."

"How about you?" I ask.

"Had to work today, mate—got down about an hour ago."

"How's it goin'—with the olds? You gonna stick at it?"

"Yeah, dough's pretty good. Why not. They're cool."

We all sit there silent for a while.

"Hi," Emy leans over and sort of whispers to me after a bit.

"Hi . . . I made it, hey."

"Yeah, thanks."

Thanks. That kind of bowls me over. I can't think of any reason she needs to say thanks to me. She's here. She came. She's beside me. Calm and true and sure, like always.

She's watching all the other guys. And watching me. "It's not real is it. It's like it can't really have happened."

"I wish it hadn't."

She's watching me.

"God, I wish it hadn't," I say again, in a soft broken voice, that maybe only I can hear.

Emy and I sit there and talk a bit. We talk about a kid who drowned in the Lane Cove River last summer—a friend of her cousin's. We talk about a kid who lived down my street who got washed off the rocks at Dee Why while he was fishing, and it was three weeks before his body came back to shore. Everyone else is so wasted it half feels like I'm alone there just with her. Dills is talking to Natalie. Emy's sort of close, sort of pulled close on her chair, moved toward me, and I feel like I just want to lean into her, touch her. Her face is soft and sad, and her long hair is falling forward. And I feel such a sad confusion. I feel like I could lean forward and hold her and kiss her and embrace her, and it would make everything else go away. I feel it would be the best thing I could ever do.

"I don't want any more to drink," I say to no one in particular. I turn to Emy. "You want to go for a walk? You want to get out of here for a bit?"

"Yeah, okay."

We get up and walk out of the beer garden. Just like that. I have this feeling like maybe there's something I should say or do first with some of the other guys, some way I should act to show how much I care. Something I should say about what we're all thinking and feeling. But I don't know what it is. I don't know how to express the emotion. And it's not quite like that. And there's this other urgency pulling at me. Just making me want to get out of there with Emy. I just want her to hold me like she did the other day on the beach, and make everything else go away.

"I never saw you at Pete's—" I say to her, as we go out of the pub and onto the street. And it occurs to me those would have to be about the dumbest words I could have possibly uttered.

"I didn't go."

I just leave it.

We go up the sidewalk outside the pub a little way, then she turns and looks at me, like she doesn't know which way I want to head.

"You want to cross over to the beach?" I ask.

"Okay."

I take her hand as we're crossing the road.

"I don't know what to say to any of the guys," I say. "I don't know what to say to you . . ."

"It doesn't matter, Matt. Just leave it until you do."

"I can't describe it . . . I didn't think anything could ever feel this bad . . ."

We walk up the beach a little.

"I don't know how it's ever going to be with Drewe and his folks again . . ."

"Oh Matt . . . you poor thing."

We walk over to the wall and start heading down to South Steyne.

"God, I didn't feel like a drink tonight," I say.

She just gives me this wistful look and then looks away, and I have this feeling she understands.

We keep walking down toward the South Steyne club house. The mist of the surf is veiled in the air along the beachfront— it hangs in yellow halos around each streetlight along the walkway.

We slow to a stop.

"Can I kiss you?"

"Uh-huh."

I put my arms around her. Feel her fine slender shape up against mine, and we don't kiss at first; I tuck my head in beside hers and my mouth is near her neck and I can sort of taste her and smell her. And I just hold her there, hug her, escape into her softness, her shape and warmth. And I start to cry, very quietly. Very still-ly. I can't stop the well of tears.

She holds me. She pulls me in closer toward her. And puts her mouth up to mine, and I feel the warm watery salt of my tears pressed between our cheeks, taste it on our lips as we kiss.

CHAPTER NINE

"THEY'RE SAYING SHE WAS DRIVING?"

"Who?"

"Here—in the paper this morning—they're saying she was driving now . . ."

"What?" I go over and look at the front page over my old man's shoulder.

We're by the balcony, at the breakfast table. Just my old man and me. It's one of those soft blue magical spring mornings. It rained overnight and everything's sweet and bright. I'm buttering toast. He's drinking coffee while he's reading the local rag.

"They're saying she had cocaine in her, but they're not saying whether there was any in Lewis Castor or not . . ." My old man puts the paper to one side and looks at me. "That surprise you, Matt?"

My old man's the coolest bastard I've ever met. He's not trying to give me a hard time. He doesn't say it in that way. He's trying to get some insight. He's trying to get a handle on what went on, on what goes on.

"Are you kidding? Hayley never used coke, Dad. Can I have a look at that?"

He hands the paper across to me. I read the story, madly, intently. The party, the crash—it's been on the front page all week. Some journo started ringing everyone up, and asking anyone he could find questions, and now Stink's party is the event of the year—the out-of-control, animal session of the decade. I stopped reading it about a day ago when it all started to become just total crap. What they don't know they're just making up.

"If they said dope, I'd say, yeah, maybe—but Hayley using coke—I can't believe it. No one I know uses coke . . . Drewe's never mentioned coke in his life . . ."

"Well, the girl was obviously doing her own thing," my old man says. And there's something amazing in the way he says that. It's like an expression of the absolute faith he has in the information I give him. It's like he has no doubt about what I'm telling him. And that's the way it's sort of built up over the years between my old man and me. It kind of worked in that inverse way—he always showed faith in the honesty of what I've told him, and that's always seemed to help me to be straight with him.

I sit there. Re-reading the story. "I can't believe this. They can't seem to work out who was driving the car now . . ."

"From what I can work out they hit that wall so hard they may never be able to work it out—no one had their belts on—and no one was left in the driver's seat . . ."

"God, this is unreal, she couldn't have been driving—Hayley didn't know how to back out of the driveway . . . Lew wouldn't be that dumb . . ."

"Well, they're talking about it . . ."

I put the paper down. It all just keeps coming at you, keeps shifting and changing. It feels like it never stops. And in the end you feel like you'll never know. Something happened, and no one was there who lived to tell the tale. And it's gone. The cops, the papers, they can try to piece it back together any way they like, but it's too late. No one will ever know, it's gone, it's over. They took it with them on the night. There was a split second or two, and someone laughed, or grabbed a steering wheel, or dropped a cigarette in their lap, or had their hand on someone else's crotch, and something happened—a pothole in the road, a flick of the wheel. Something happened in a split second. And the car tore along the rock wall so hard that it literally peeled the side off it. And it sounded to the people that lived in the houses nearby like screaming metal. But by then it was over. The split second of what really happened, was finished. Gone. And all we get after that is stories and reconstructions and crap. But it doesn't really matter. All that matters, has happened—and it's over. What is left can only ever be "after the fact." I'm after the fact now. Hayls' old lady and old man are after the fact. Lew's folks and friends are all left behind, and way after the fact. We're all after the "what really happened." Then the cops and the papers start talking—start talking it up and around—about how wild the whole scene was, about all the shit everyone was supposedly shooting and snorting and ripping into, and it all starts to have a life of its own—and if you were there, it starts to look less and less like what really went on. It gets so that you can barely recognize it. But it's all over. It's just stories. What happened—happened before the stories.

I give the paper back to my old man. It's fucking mad, but I can see it now. Hayley coaxing some coke out of one of the *edge* crowd at school, just for a lark. Hayley coaxing Lew to let her drive the Boxster. And it all going wrong, by some mad fluke. Hayley losing control, Hayley hitting the accelerator instead of the brake. For just a second I get a flash in my head of that instant of devastation. That mad closing-in of the horrific, the incredible, that night. It's like a cold daylight nightmare. It's enough to make you scream out. In the bitterest way, it makes sense for the first time since it all happened. Lew could never be so reckless and dangerous.

My old man's watching me. Reading my face.

"So what do you think, Matt?"

"Anything's possible."

"It's awful tragic."

"Yeah." And I feel the water welling behind my eyes like it

just keeps doing these last few days. It's all over, but it's never over.

"It's all right, mate," my dad says.

"Yeah, Dad."

The next day I go in for my op. I catch the bus real early over to Royal North Shore. My old lady wants to drive me, but I just want to get there alone, and get on with it. I let her know I'm not trying to give her a hard time, and she's cool about it. She's not the same since Hayley died. She's hanging back a bit more. An exactness, a sureness has been peeled away from her manner. I walk up to the hospital from the highway in the early morning and they show me to the orthopedic ward. I sit on a bed and read the morning paper until a nurse who's probably about five years older than me comes along and shaves the bottom half of my legs for the op. She's a real honey. She's chatting and raving the whole time she's doing it. Then when she's finished she calls a couple of other nurses over, and she says, "Look at his legs! How come the guys always have the best legs!" They all carry on. They're all crazy. But she's a real hoot. She cheers me up a little, 'cause I'm feeling a little down.

A little after nine the doc comes around to check me out. He tells me how they really have to put me under 'cause some of the work in the op is a little heavy duty, and how the knockout's going to make me feel a little spewy for a while when I wake up. He also lets me know they have to put a metal pin in each foot to hold the joint in place while it's healing after the op. I just sit there and nod. I'm not feeling any uncertainty or last-minute fear or desire to get out of there. Lately the discomfort's sort of carried me past that. It's like when you walk in and you say "Just fix it—I don't give a stuff about the rest." Well, that's how I'm feeling. My feet are bugging me all the time now, almost every day. I'm just looking forward to a day after the op and none of it's there anymore. I'm kind of dreaming of that day. If the doc said, "Right, Matt, we'll just be sawing each foot off this morning" I'd probably just sit there and nod.

They put me in a gown with my arse hanging out, and I go up a corridor and take a pee. Then they give me some shots to put me under. Last thing I remember I'm flat on my back sailing down these corridors with rows of lights flickering by overhead like sleepers on a railway line—going on forever and ever. Then it all starts to melt and slide away to the sides, and that's it.

On Sunday I'm still on the ward. I'm eating chicken drum-sticks for dinner and Drewe wanders in.

"Up and hobbling yet, ya creaky old bastard?"

"Fuck yeah."

"How are ya?"

"Okay. They didn't have to remove the head."

"That's a bonus."

"Yeah, coulda been worse. What's news?"

"Well, the shit really blew—they reckon they were both zipped on coke—and they reckon Hayley was driving . . ."

"Bullcrap . . . I just can't fucking believe that . . ."

"That's what the cops reckon—they've done the big report."

"You seen it?"

"Yeah—I've seen it. I sat with the old man in the solicitor's office while he went through it and explained it to us."

"No shit—"

"Yeah. Little Sis went out in party mode."

"Where the fuck did she get it?"

"Who knows—but that's no major issue."

"Unreal. I just can't fuckin' believe it."

"Yeah . . . well . . ." he says, and his gaze drifts away to nowhere in particular as he's caught by the drag of his thoughts. "She always did have a bit of a taste for the glam, mate . . ." He sits on the edge of the bed, but doesn't look at me. He has that dazed look of not quite comprehending. "You know, Matt . . . it's like I haven't had a chance to feel any of this yet . . . to register it. It's like it's all happened too fast." He sighs, so sadly. "With Hayley—you know—how do you say it? She could drive you absolutely nuts. She could send you right around the fucking bend—but we were *so close*. When we grew up, we were like one thing—always fighting and carrying on and giving each other and everyone else heaps—Christ, we used to fight and we'd tear hunks out of each other's hair." He stops and looks down at his upturned hand with the recollection of her hair clenched in it. "But even with all that mad shit we were still always so close—we knew all the same kids, we lived all the same stuff—we were like a little *whole*. How do you say that thing, that way someone drove you nuts, but you loved them so much too? You almost feel you loved them more because of the way they used to do such a good job of shaking your tree. 'Cause they never stopped coming at you, 'cause they always had the spine to be themselves even in the face of a big brother." He gives a little gasp of sadness at the recognition of what he's said. "I've lost a part of my whole world, mate." He looks over at me. "A part of everything I am . . ."

I just sit there, and hold the water in my eyes. And think how he got at a truth we both know.

I sit there a little longer, without speaking. And then I start to think about this thing with the coke. I feel like I couldn't know less. I feel like I never knew anything. I was spinning out over Hayley and I just didn't have a clue. I didn't really know a thing about where she was at.

"Lew using coke," I say, "I still can't believe that. The guy'd pull up after two middies of light 'cause he reckoned it was getting too heavy . . ."

"Spot on. Don't ask me. I don't know what the hell went on." Drewe pauses. He looks a little unsure. Then he says. "They did the full bit, you know—an autopsy or whatever . . ."

"Yeah?"

"Don't tell this to another soul, right . . ."

"Yeah."

"And he had coke on his dick . . ."

I just look back at him dumbly.

"Makes you last longer, they reckon. Makes you last forever . . ."

I'm still looking back at him, struck dumb.

"Too many copies of *Cleo*, mate." He makes a face like having encountered the stupendous. Then he says, "The cops talked to the old man—they said they'd leave a few things out of the report . . ."

"Chriiisst . . ." I just say softly, dragging it out. "Did they fuck?"

"Yeah—reckon so."

Drewe draws back. Just sits there, checking me out. "So what do you know?" he says after a while.

"Sweet FA, obviously."

"My old man punched out some journo. Fairly put his Nikon halfway back into his brain. Bastard ended up in Manly Hospital—as if anyone cares . . . The guy just wouldn't give up—kept coming around to the door at all sorts of stupid hours—and my old lady's cracking up badly. The cops didn't care shit—he tried to make a report, and when they found out what it was about they told him to piss off."

"How's your mum?"

"Not good, mate. I'm just doing everything I can . . . I'm just trying to be there heaps . . ."

We sit there for a moment and I think about life. About the way stuff happens and the weird way it changes you. You don't feel any different. But you are. You look for the scars and the broken bones—but they're not there, they're somewhere else. It comes at you in some other way.

It's funny how we think our world isn't going to change. You wonder where it comes from, such a bald, ridiculous belief in the opposite of what's so certain. Perhaps it's only when you're so young that you can have such easy faith in what's so ridiculous. Or maybe not. Maybe that's how we all continue. All along, through the course of our lives. Maybe that's how we keep going.

I look at Drewe. "So what's happening with you? What's happening with Layla?"

"She's not talking to me."

"What's that mean?"

"It means I go around there and try to talk to her and her old lady tells me she's not in. But I got her on the phone the other day and told her I wanted her to keep it—I told her I'd look after it . . ."

"So what'd she say?"

"She said she didn't know."

"You afraid she's going to have an abortion?"

"Yeah, sorta."

"If she hasn't already?"

"Yeah—if she hasn't already. But I don't think she has."

"Her olds know?"

"No—and I'm not letting on. Or that would really fuck things. It's just between her and me."

I sit. And think about what's been going on. "Fuck, mate—what happened?"

He's still sitting on the edge of the bed. "You said it, mate—the sky fell in." He looks over at my feet under the covers. "How you feeling?"

"Bit sore. But I've got pain-killers to the eyeballs."

"I'll bet. Scraped the bone, hey—is that what you said?"

"Yeah. Something like that."

"Sounds like a real party."

"Yeah, tops."

"So when you bustin' out?"

"Soon as I can hobble to the loo and back is the word from the physio—she reckons I'll be right for tomorrow."

"So when you good for a wave then?"

"Faaark—I don't know—don't give me a hard time . . . I don't know if I'm ever going to be good for a wave again. I've been thinking, maybe I'll start out on a lid and go from there . . ."

"A *lid*! A fucking *shark biscuit*, mate! Are you having me on? Death before dishonor, mate. I see you out in the surf on a fucking lid, mate, I'll run you over personally."

"Thanks, mate. Always nice to know who's looking out for ya."

"Fucken A. And don't you forget it."

We sit there.

"Life's fucked, mate."

"No it's not," Drewe says. "God was out at North Curly this morning, mate. Was up at five—hadn't had a decent wave for ages—got down there—light's just breaking. And I'm up on the dunes checkin' it out. And God's out there—hangin' back and takin' a long line, strokin' his beard as he's settin' it up on a big crystal wall. Watched from the top of the dunes for a bit—then when I got out there he was gone . . ."

I smile. It's an old joke of ours. There used to be a big poster down at Manly Surf Shop. It was there all the years we were growing up, learning to surf. Pic of an old guy with a big beard on a mal, set up on a long, long beautiful wall, just hanging there, cruising. And down the bottom it said something like, "If there's a God—he surfs." It was always a favorite of mine. I used to rave to Drewe about it.

I feel a welling of sadness. I feel a sense of something lost. Drewe knows the God's a surfer routine is one of my favorites. "Yeah, he always splits early," I say. I think about getting back out in the water. It's like a far-off, perfect dream in my head. It gives me hope.

"Got to go, mate—had any other visitors?"

"Just the folks—this afternoon. Haven't told anyone else I'm in here. Didn't want to make a big deal of it."

He looks suddenly quiet. "The funeral's Friday, okay—the Anglican Chapel at the Northern Suburbs Crematorium—I dropped a note up to your old lady this afternoon. You going to be all right for that?"

"Yeah. I'll be all right."

"I can't give you a ride, mate. I've got to be with the olds."

"Yeah, I know."

He's about to go but he waits, 'cause he knows I'm about to speak.

"I'm scared shitless about seeing them, you know, mate. I'm totally fucked up about it."

"Mate, you wouldn't be anything else."

"I was supposed to look after their daughter . . ."

"You did, mate . . ."

"No I didn't—that's total bullshit. I didn't look after her. I didn't look out for her. I didn't do a fucking thing."

"That's crap."

"Well, it's how I feel."

"Listen, Matt. I'm her brother. If I thought that, I'd let you know. Hayley did her own thing . . ."

"Well, I wish she hadn't . . ."

"We all wish she hadn't, mate . . . Listen, when you see the olds—just be cool. Just hang cool. They know you did what you could."

"Yeah, okay."

"See ya, mate."

"Yeah."

I lie there, thinking about it after he's gone, and then I do a trial hobble up to the loo with my two canes—keeping my weight on my heels like the physio's shown me. There's no remedy for it I think. I feel like I understand what people mean now when they say only time can fix something. There's no other remedy for any of this.

Late Monday morning, my old man drives over and picks me up and takes me home. The pretty nurse who reckons I've got such great legs, and I'm half in love with, brings a wheelchair and won't let me out of the place till I sit down and shut up and get into it. She says as soon as I get out of the grounds I can fall flat on my face for all she cares, but while I'm in there and on my way out, I have to sit in the chair. Hospital policy, risk management, some crap like that. My old man walks beside us carrying my bag, not saying a thing, checking me and this nurse out and listening to the banter, as she wheels me out into the bright, clear day, and I catch the heady scent of the frangipanis that line the path as we go down to the parking lot.

As we go through St. Leonards I'm sitting in the front seat studying the bright blue of the sky through the windscreen. And now and then I look down at the two canes at one side, and my feet wrapped thickly in bandages with the tips of my toes coming out the end, and a steel pin protruding out the tip of each big toe. I'm starting to wonder when and how the hell they're going to get those pins out.

"How they feel?" my old man asks, watching me, as he drives.

"All right—bit tender."

"Bound to be. Take it easy for a while, hey—no booting the ball around the backyard, huh."

I give a cracked sort of a laugh. It's almost funny.

CHAPTER TEN

WE BURY HAYLEY IN THE HEAT. AND I'M WALKING with two canes. It's one of those spring days when the temperature amps up like a furnace. A big blowy stifling nor'wester comes up out of the inland. Nine in the morning and it's melting things, making things wilt, blowing in your face, filling your mouth, drying a dust on your skin—it's all around you and you can't escape it. I go out to the crematorium with Dills. "Sad day, mate," he says, as we're driving out there. "Sad day. This is the baddest shit . . ." He pauses. "My little sister was in her year you know . . . Reckons she didn't really know her though . . ."

And it's so hot. The heat does something to the occasion somehow. It makes it so stark, so striking, it's like we're all standing too near to the furnace.

We park where all the cars park, and then go and stand in the crowd out the front of the chapel with our sunglasses on in the heat. Everyone's there but no one's talking. The day is so pale and stark and bright it draws something away. You don't want to talk. You're trying not to fade. I hang there on my canes. I won't sit down. I find if I balance flat on my feet they feel all right. I slit some runners open so I could get my bandaged feet into them. The swelling's gone down heaps—but it was still pretty tight. I check out the crowd—there's a little group chucking poses, that look like a pack of wankers for a Ray Ban ad, and because of them I take my sunglasses off. Hayley's olds aren't there, Drewe's not there. I don't really know what goes on. So I just wait, in the white light. Then a white hearse pulls up driven by a lady in a white suit, and there's another lady inside in white with a crimson hat, and Drewe and his folks pull up right after in a white car that stops behind.

I stand and watch as Drewe and his old man and the two ladies in white take the coffin out of the hearse. I start crying right then, very stiffly, very quietly, and I can't stop it, no matter how much I want to. It's the last thing I wanted to do. But it just takes me over. It just comes at me and I can't hold it off. A thick grief that closes off my throat, a well of sadness I can't hold down. I watch Drewe go by, with his long hair looking wet and tied back in a ponytail and he's got a suit on, and his old man's on the other side and I can't really see him. And Hayley's schoolmates come forward in a wave in their summer dresses and start throwing flowers on the coffin as they carry it by, and there's the soft bright blur of color of the thudding rain of the flowers. And I think to myself, I didn't think to bring any flowers. And after the coffin's gone by Hayley's old lady is walking behind, and her face is so torn up and she's crying, and she sees me and her eyes don't leave me, and as she gets to me she says, "Oh Matt," in the softest, faintest voice, "if only she'd stayed with you." She says it through her muffled soft trauma. And I swear it's the last thing I wanted to hear anyone say. And I stand there, standing up in the bright white heat with my two canes, crying, and then the crowd starts to follow the coffin inside, and I pull out of the way 'cause I'm afraid my feet are going to get stepped on.

I go in last. And find a seat by myself over on the edge of the aisle on the left near the wall. They begin the service and I sort of listen, then after a little while I realize there's a bird up in the roof somewhere—there's been these sort of birdlike noises going on all along. And I don't really hear much of the service 'cause I'm so upset and I can't seem to stop it. Hayley's old man says something after the minister and it just makes me choke up more, then Drewe says something and I'm still trying to stop crying, and all the time this bird is chirping and flying around high up in the chapel between the beautiful polished wood beams and the open white ceiling and the bright flood of light through stained glass.

And then it's over, and they're carrying the coffin back out, and Hayley's mates from her school are still throwing flowers.

And I just feel so worked over and exhausted and pounded. And looking into the colored swirl of petals falling, I think about Hayley. Think about her for the first time in a little while—in a way that feels different. She drifts across my mind, sharp and alive and distinct, and she seems almost there, her presence is so clear in my head. I sense that sure exterior of hers, that perfect sheen of beauty—that was almost like a flower's in its sheerness, in its velvety exquisiteness. But my mind doesn't catch on that, it slips away into a thought about her essence. That way she was, that pushing heart of hers. That's what I loved more than anything about Hayley, that way she *was*. That strange fierceness in her. Her casual brown beauty, had only ever been an add-on, just the killer blow.

And I stand there still, as the tail end of the crowd is shuffling out, and think about all that. All that *fire* and *want*. That inexplicable way she *attracted*. And how it has all been extinguished. How it will never be again. How it will never get to be *more*. And that's the part that's most crushing in me. What I played a part in taking away. Hayley didn't get what she wanted. Hayley didn't get what she should have. Hayley didn't get what she deserved. She was denied. She was refused. She was taken by *mad* life. And that's what's really breaking me up in the worst way now. Not that I didn't mean a rats to her—and I had to stop kidding myself and come to terms with that. But that she didn't get to go on and be what she might have. Be all the things she could have. She didn't get to *become*.

I stand there, and think of that. Of what's lost. What's taken.

What will be forever missing. Hayley was denied. I wipe my eyes again. And then I follow the last of the people back out into the light that blinds us as we hit the door, and the heat that rushes into our faces.

It's a strange sort of process. Everyone gets back in their cars that are as hot as ovens, and the hearse waits for a bit, then the cars follow the hearse a short way up the road in a long creeping line to the crematorium.

"You all right, mate?" Dills says.

"Yeah," I say, wiping my face. "I didn't think I'd get so upset . . ."

"It's all right, mate . . ."

It's kind of a traffic jam, getting out of the parking lot by the chapel, but the cars gradually crawl out, and Dills just waits, saying nothing more than "God, it's hot" a couple of times. Then we get on about the very end of the line of cars.

We creep up to the crematorium, with the slow crunch of gravel under our tires. My feet are generating a dull warmth. No pain, but a heat. I open my window wider, the dry air billows in. "Never thought I'd be so pissed to see an off-shore," I say.

Dills cracks a faint smile.

"Hear all this about the coke?" he says after a minute.

"Yeah . . . Drewe told me . . ."

Dills has got both hands resting at the top of the steering wheel. "Remember Spears' brother's mate—Rymer? Got done for knocking off cars?"

"Yeah."

"He was always doing a line."

"Yeah?"

"Used to piss on something fierce all night—then have a big snort to drive home. Reckoned it straightened you right out—blew all the piss out of your system."

"No shit."

"Yeah. I was with him and Spears once—we're going up through the Spit Ss—pretty late, after the pub—going over to some party in Mosman—and he's freakin' me out the way he's drivin'—he's all over the place. And I said something about maybe he's too pissed to drive, and he comes back with how he's had a nose full and it straightens you right out. Thing was—the bastard wasn't even fuckin' half straight. Just seemed to think he was . . ."

"Yeah . . . it's like that, hey?"

"Yeah. This guy was wacked. He nearly totaled us all."

"You reckon Lew would use coke?"

He lets out a long sigh before he answers. "No—not at ten on a Saturday morning—or eight on a Friday night . . . But two in the morning, burning around in the old man's Porsche with Hayley Churchill with her lips around your dick . . . anything's possible . . ." He looks over at me. "Sorry, mate, no offense."

"Yeah . . ."

At the crematorium we park at the end of a line of cars in the green black shadows under a great line of trees. As we're getting out of the car Dills says, "How the feet handling it, mate?"

"Yeah, they're holding up. Don't reckon I'm on for a wave this afternoon though."

He laughs. "Forget it—it's flat."

"Yeah? Check it out, hey?"

"Yeah. Drove by . . . had a look."

We cross the red gravel of the car park and follow the crowd inside the crematorium. The crematorium's cool inside like a cave—all heavy draped scarlet velvet curtains and muted lights behind panels. The white coffin is sitting up on a sort of runway and the minister's out the front again and he says a few more words. It's not like in the chapel earlier. It's all dim and subdued and muted now. There's no bird larking about up high in the bright airy ceiling. The coffin starts to roll and someone starts to howl and I can't make out if it's Hayley's old lady or one of her schoolmates—I can't really see, the bodies are really packed in there. And the coffin trundles slowly in through the little sliding door and the door starts to slide shut after it and the curtains are being drawn and I can't see the inferno down the line but I crane my neck trying to get a look at it as it goes. As we all do.

I stand in the back of the dim hall as the crowd files out again into the white spring light, and I wait there and have a vision of a pale plume of smoke rising in a puff above the tall stack of the crematorium. It's only my vision. I don't know if it happens like that or not, but it's what gets in my head.

When I get outside, it's like there's a queue. Mr. and Mrs. Churchill are standing over under a tree on the other side of the red gravel lot, and it seems a line of people has formed to give them their condolences. Call me weird, but it's not where I want to go. It's a long line of people, probably all a bit too flipped out and upset right then to bother stopping and thinking about what they're doing—and whether it's going to give Hayley's olds any joy or not. I know it probably wasn't meant to be like that, it probably just started up 'cause a couple of people wanted to say something to them and went over, and then a couple more waited while the ones in front finished, and the next thing you know you got a line there or something, but I can't bring myself to get on the end of a queue.

"My feet are stuffed," I say to Dills as we come out. "I gotta go sit down for a bit."

I go over and sit on the steps in the shade at the side of the entrance to the crematorium. He goes off and joins the line. I watch him trudge away across the red gravel. I look around. There's the line, and there's people all over the place. There's little clusters of Hayley's mates scattered in groups of three and four around the car park in their bright summer dresses, with their sunglasses on and their hankies pressed to their faces. I like the dresses. It's like a kind of statement about life, about the beauty and the vivacity of Hayley, about the joy of spring—it's like some expression of belief. But I'm not sure if it's what Hayley would have done. Hayley would have worn black, or dark, dark brown to a funeral, I reckon, and looked like a fuckin' goddess and every guy there wouldn't have been able to take his eyes off her. I watch the crowd. There's guys from down the beach, a heap of them—all the crew and more, other guys that Drewe knows; there's Hayley's folks' friends and rellies. It's a lot of people, and it can't help but make you wonder where you fit in. Then I remember where I fit in—I'm the guy that took her to the party. I'm the guy that got her out from under the nose of her olds.

"Matt."

I look up, it's Emy.

"Hi," I say.

"Hello," she says, and sits down beside me on the low step. She's got on a brown dress and black shoes. And I'm thinking to myself, I know it's Hayley's funeral but she looks so sexy. Whoever thought a babe could look so good all in chocolate brown. You can't work it out what babes do.

She looks at my feet in the cut runners. "I wish you'd told me, about going into hospital . . . I would have been cool . . ."

" . . . Yeah . . . I know . . . I'm sorry. I'm so pissed off and screwed up about all this stuff with my feet. I couldn't handle it . . . I didn't really tell anyone. I just went off and did it."

She gives me a funny appraising look, like that makes total sense to her.

"Everything go okay?"

"Yeah, fine."

We sit there for a bit, and then I say, "It's sort of an arthritis—it was getting really sore sometimes . . ." And I swear, it nearly kills me to get that out. But I wrench it free of all that stuff that hangs back in me. I speak the words out loud to her. Because it's Emy. Because I want to. I want to tell her about it. And then I sort of grin inside 'cause it occurs to me maybe I'm not up for half as much therapy as I probably needed before. "Sorry . . ." I say to her.

"It's cool," she says. "No one ever wants to talk about stuff like that . . ."

We sit there quiet again for a moment, and watch all the people.

"I haven't seen Lew's olds," I say.

"They may not be coming."

"What's up?"

"It got a bit ugly . . ."

"Yeah? What happened?"

"They said something—and it got in the newspaper . . . sort of like their son got led astray . . ."

We sit in silence.

"He never did much shit, you know."

"That's sort of what they were on about. Raine showed it to me . . . when the police report came out some journo phoned them up . . . and they made a few comments . . ."

"Oh fuck. And Hayley's old man gave 'em a blast in reply did he?"

"Yeah, pretty much."

"Well, he would."

She gazes around. "This is the weirdest place."

"Shit, isn't it."

I look around some more.

"Yeah, I don't think it's the way I want to go. I want to be rolled off a deck smack into the middle of the ocean . . ."

"Mmm . . . for the fish to nibble on . . . or maybe dug in under the rosebushes at the top of our garden." She smiles and pauses, and looks down at her dress.

I watch her. "You look beautiful, you know."

"Why, thank you. Just don't try and kiss me."

I grin. I swear all babes ever do is give me a hard time.

"I wasn't going to."

She smiles. "Well, not now anyway."

We sit there some more, just watching.

"My grandad died last year, you know," she says.

"Yeah."

"He was eighty-two. He'd been all over the world—building bridges, putting tunnels through mountains—he was an engineer. He'd married twice, and he had like fifteen grandkids. But after he was gone . . . you wonder what it was all about." She turns to me. "You know the thing I mean."

"Yeah . . ."

We fall quiet again. There's a little crowd right in front of us. A girl in a yellow dress and a black hat is talking loudly. Another is laughing.

"But it's not like that for Hayley . . ." I say.

"No . . ."

We pause.

"I've got to talk to her olds, but I don't know what to say."

"Tell them how much you loved her."

And right then, Hayley's old man is there.

He's come up, and he's standing right there in front of me. I haven't even seen him coming, because I've been kind of looking down at the ground or something when I'm talking to Emy. And I look up, and he's just there. And I get up sort of too quick, and forget my feet, and a shot of pain flashes through them, courses right up through me, just as I'm up and he's reaching out to me. Holding out his hand.

And he's a big guy. He's always been a big guy. One of these big, brick-wide, thick-forearmed guys. And he takes my hand, then he pulls me into him, and doesn't let me go for a bit. He just holds me there, and I hold him. Then he lets me go, but he's still holding my hand.

We stand there looking at each other for a second. We're both crying. Then at last he speaks.

"I know you're upset, Matt. We're all upset. But come down to the house sometime, hey . . . like you've always done . . . come and sit at the kitchen table and have a chat . . . like always . . . tell us what you've been up to . . ."

I'm crying. And I can't talk for a bit. But then I manage to say, "Yeah, Mr. Churchill . . . I will."

And he's still holding my hand.

"I loved her, Mr. Churchill . . . I'm so sorry . . ." I just manage to get it out, before it all floods in my head so bad I can't speak again.

"We know, Matt. We know." And he lets go my hand, and just stands there for a minute, kind of looking at me, kind of not looking at me. Wiping the tears from his eyes.

"I watched you guys, you know, Matt. I watched you grow up . . . And I thought my job was pretty much done. I thought I'd just about done the job . . ." But he can't go on. "We love you, son . . . just be a friend to Drewe . . ."

"I will, Mr. Churchill."

And we both stand there crying again.

And then he turns and goes. Slowly. Sort of moving stiff and shaky with his grief and his age back across the gravel.

I just stand there for a little longer. Then I kind of slowly lower myself back down. And as I sit, I shift the two canes a little—that were beside me on the step; adjust their place just a little, to steady my emotions, to steady the world. Then I sit there, still, for a while. Feeling the hot dry wind whipping around me. Drying the water on my face.

After a while Emy gets up. And I get up too. Some of the cars have started to leave. Other people are still wandering around talking.

"I would have come to see you in hospital," she says.

"Yeah I know . . ."

She smiles. "You got my number?"

"Yeah."

"You going to use it?"

"Yeah . . ."

"Don't wait too long, hey. I don't care if you can't dance."

"Maybe we'll go for a swim, hey. I could probably handle that."

"Me too." She stands there looking at me. "I've got to go."

"Okay."

And she goes away from me. Over to some crowd of babes I don't know in her brown dress I like so much even though I'm at a funeral. There's no accounting for attraction, for the effect of a babe on a guy. I reckon you could be at your own mother's funeral and if some sort caught your eye you'd still be checking her out. Maybe it's the age I'm at, I don't know.

Dills comes back.

"Saw you talking to Drewe's old man."

"Yeah."

"How'd it go?"

"Pretty cool." I could almost laugh out loud at myself sometimes.

Dills is surveying the crowd as he listens. "Check out this sort in the red dress," he says. "What a honey."

"Yeah, mate. Let's go, hey."

CHAPTER ELEVEN

WHEN YOU SURF, YOU PASS THROUGH A VORTEX. YOU pull into a wave, and go in one end, and come out the other, and it's brief and fast and furious—and it flashes by you so fierce and wondrous that most of the time you barely know what's happened. It's gone by, before you can believe it. It's over, before you've barely had a chance to *realize* it in your head. And you're left so rolled over, and blown away. You're left so wondering—you scarcely know. You scarcely know what's happened.

I can't tell you how I learned about things. The way I found out that nothing's guaranteed. I can't tell you how deep that runs now. Hayley was divine, Hayley was perfect. Hayley was bound to go on and be something. Be more than any of us; out in the great world. Everyone knew that. Everyone said that. But we were wrong. We were all wrong. None of it was certain. And now I know that.

In the days after Hayley's funeral, I fall into a bit of a hole. The vortex closes in on me a little, and I do a stupid thing. I don't go to Lew's funeral. I should have. But I don't. In those couple of days I seem to slip into the most awful kind of place. Something dreadful rises up in me, and takes over me. Something defeated and pained and so crushed with futility, that for a while, just then, I can't seem to bear to do anything at all. So I don't go. But I regret not going to Lew's funeral almost straight after. I had no real issue with Lew. It was all past *fault* for me. All that meant nothing to me. He'd been a friend of mine. I'd known him for a long time. And I wish I'd gone. But after I missed it, it almost seems the recognition of that regret, of the dumbness of what I've done, helps to steer me out of the way I feel. Helps to push me forward a little. Because it passes, it falls from me. And I'm glad. Because if I hadn't come back from that impact point of pain, if I'd stayed there too long. I don't know how it would be. I could see how it could wreck you. How you could haunt yourself forever.

A couple of days after Lew's, Drewe drops up to see me. We're sitting in the living room. I've been hanging on the sofa all morning, reading the papers, watching the tube, looking out the window—it feels all right now, just doing nothing for a while. I feel a strange sort of faith in something—in the future—and I don't know where it springs from. But that doesn't matter. I feel like one day some of the better stuff will be back, and I'll be okay again. Each day my feet are a little less sore. And for the moment I don't mind hanging around doing nothing. It's like a break from the deluge of life that seemed to happen. I think I can even bear a break from the surf. I'm content just to be nowhere for a bit.

Drewe rocks in and starts changing channels and picking out riffs on the six-string, then he goes and raids our cupboards and comes back with a bag of chips. I tell him to go for it, Delia's not home.

"Want me to tell you about the surf, mate?"

"No—bugger off—I didn't even look out the window this morning."

"No surf today, mate—it's flat."

"Oh crap—three to four from the southeast—faintest fuckin' nor'easter—North Steyne, Longey, North Narra. I'd go North Narra. It'd be fuckin' magic."

"I did." He just laughs, still stuffing chips in his face. "Not suffering, hey mate . . . So how long till you're wiggling your toes?"

"Two weeks—they're pulling the pins."

"That'll be a hoot."

"Real blast. Went in for a check-up yesterday."

"Yeah? Everything cool?"

"Yeah. Seems to be."

"Good stuff. You'll be kickin' the cat again before you know it."

"The doc keeps telling me it's going to take a while—reckons it'll be months . . ."

"Yeah, reckon it will."

Drewe sits down and seems to quieten abruptly.

"It's going to take a hell of a lot longer to get over the rest, mate," he says suddenly

"Oh yeah," I say softly.

I look over at him. "I think about Hayls all the time, you know—like she's still here. I think I'll say something to her, when I see her at your place . . . or if I catch her down the beach. You can't seem to help it, can you."

He looks at me. "You were like us, Matt—you loved her . . ."

"Yeah. I don't know why . . ."

"There never is a reason, mate. Someone should have told you that."

I just check him out. I don't have anything to say.

"Layla's having the baby," he says. "She's having *our* baby. I was going to say she's having *my* baby, but faaark, if I go around saying that I'll never hear the end of it . . ."

"No shit. What happened?"

"I don't know what happened in the end. I'd given up trying. Then she calls me up and says to come around and see her. And I do, and we sit in the lounge and have a cup of tea and a biscuit and she tells me there's no way we're getting married or any bullshit like that, but she wants to have the baby. And that's it. And I just say, well, that's cool with me—I want to have it too. So that's where it's at."

"Yeah? So what'll happen?"

"Don't know yet. But she's told her olds and a few other people and she's officially pregnant now."

"Fuck, who'd pick it. You told your old man yet?"

"Not yet. I just want it to get a little further down the line first."

"Reckon he'll be cool?"

"I reckon he'll spew—he's never been cool in his life."

"Yeah he has. He was cool with me."

Drewe just checks me out. And doesn't say anything to that.

"Anyway, there'll be heaps of people to look after the bubs—we'll just work it out as we go—me, Layla, my olds, Layla's olds—we'll work it out as we go . . ."

"Poor kid, won't know where it's at."

"Well, that only puts it at risk of ending up like you—"

"Thanks, mate."

"No sweat. I've run out of insults—I'm pissing off. Tell your old lady she needs to do some shopping."

"Love to."

"Come down for a game of pool later in the week?"

"You mean your place?"

"Yeah."

"Yeah, okay. I'll try."

"Don't *try* mate. Just front. I'll call ya. I'll come and pick ya up."

He stops and looks at me. "It's cool, mate . . . you can do it."

I look back at him, and just nod.

I hobble to the door with him. I've given the canes the flick. I fuckin' hated the things. The doc reckons I should have a half decent sort of walk going in a couple of weeks.

"Keep doin' your chin-ups, hey mate," Drewe says, as he slips out.

In the end, I search myself for clear feeling, for understanding, but I never seem to know what I feel. Things happen, and you have this notion they'll make you feel this way, they'll change you that way. But it just doesn't seem to be like that. It all just seems to spin you in some way you never conceived of. You react, you wear it, and you surprise yourself as you watch yourself. I want to say something true about Hayley, but I can't seem to. I can't reconcile it all, the way I felt for her, and the way she didn't feel for me, and all the other shit that went on. I guess I'll never be able to put it together into a smooth package. I'll just have to learn to live with it the way it was.

I miss Hayley though. I miss her so much some days. I used to walk down the hill just to see her. I'd call up Drewe and go around and see him, just in the hope of running into Hayley. But she's not there anymore. Not anymore. Hayley's gone. Like the way when you're out in the surf real early sometimes and you watch the sun rise out of the water. And then it's gone. Up into the sky. There's a brief blur of beauty that is astounding. Then it's gone. And it can be so fleeting. You can miss it.

**As many as one in three
Americans with HIV...
DO NOT KNOW IT.**

**More than half of those
who will get HIV this year...
ARE UNDER 25.**

**HIV is preventable.
You can help fight AIDS.
Get informed. Get the facts.**

**www.knowhivaids.org
1-866-344-KNOW**